MW01128907

Copyright 2012 Thea Atkinson

Published by Thea Atkinson
Cover photo by Dreamtwist
Cover design by Thea Atkinson

Chapter 1

The call of a vulture was the sound that brought Alaysha back.

It was always the shriek of the carrion bird that brought her around afterwards, like the sacred minerals tribal shamans used to bring a dream-walker back to reality. It wasn't as though she fainted during battle—would to the Deities she could—but rather, she sort of went into herself and hid there, somewhere inside, while the deed was done. After all these years, she supposed her psyche had trained itself to recover only when it heard the sure signs of scavenge and she could know it was over.

She dreaded the sound of the vulture like a dying man would, except for different reasons: while the dying dreaded the sound of imminent death, it reminded her that she still lived.

With reluctant dread she opened her eyes and let go a gust of breath. Without thinking, she turned in the direction of the bird's call. It was off to the left, circling over a copse of trees. She kept her gaze on the bird, knowing it would circle ever closer to her, bringing with it a brood of others to worry fruitlessly at the bodies littered across the now arid land in front of her. Still, watching the scavenger was far better than facing what she knew was in front of her. Infinitely better, too, than turning to what would wait behind her.

They would be coming soon.

She let her gaze travel from the broad wings of the carrion bird to the grove of trees beneath that were still lush and vibrant. Strange, how a small oasis of vegetation could be left at all, but there it was. She judged the distance to be at least one hundred horse strides away. So, the power still had its limits then. She did some quick calculations: a few hundred paces short of a leagua? Could that be right? If she remembered accurately, the last time she'd done battle, the line of growth had started just short of a kubit. She'd ridden it afterwards and counted the beats of her mount's hooves to be certain: five hundred horse strides at full gallop, so yes, a kubit if anything, but three times that much?

She measured the breadth of the distance with her eyes, imagining herself atop Barruch's back, his mane in her face as he galloped, measuring with breathless counts: one stride, two strides, three. This time the line seemed pressed back, almost a blur on the horizon. So it seemed that, although the power had limits, it was growing.

How long would it be before she couldn't see vegetation at all?

Best not to think about it. They would be here soon, inspecting her work, making sure each enemy and each child, grandchild, and friend of the enemy was gone. And the price of that annihilation was the loss of the very fluid that lent life to the area before she'd come.

She sighed and scanned the few hundred mount strides before her. Nothing but arid sand and crackled, dried out soil. The trees had become tinder on vertical stalks. It wasn't a desert by any stretch, but the vegetation had crinkled to dust and creatures of all sorts had fallen like apples from the trees to their bases. What grass or moss or shrubberies that had padded her bare feet when she'd climbed down from her mount and sent him with a slap back towards her camp, was now dust beneath her soles and dried husks of fiber beside her.

She knew without checking that the destruction went beneath her feet as well. If it stretched out for a leagua in all directions, it certainly went at least a quarter as deep into the ground.

The only thing belying the dryness was the cloud cover. So dense and broodingly heavy with water, it darkened the sky. The rain would come soon; the clouds wouldn't be able to hold themselves together under the weight of the water that fattened them. The lightning, too. Sparking the tinder of trees and shrubs, lighting the area with a blaze fierce, but temporary at best in the face of the inevitable downpour.

And then it would seem as if nothing had ever lived.

It didn't matter she'd been doing this since she'd been old enough to sit in a basket hanging from the side of her father's mount, she could never get over the sense of desolation left in her wake.

Water witch. It was a bastardized term that came from her mother's old tongue that, she had learned somewhere along the way, had originated as temptress of the life blood. She much preferred the original form to the bastardized phrase her father's people had begun to use long before her sixth birthday. That version, and the way they spat it out was filled with contempt. And fear. So much fear, even she began to understand why they ostracized her so.

At first, she'd thought it was because of her mother. Then she thought it was because of her father. Only when she gained her moon's blood in her twelfth season did she realize that both of those things were the most true.

The sound of horse hooves behind her stole her attention from the wasteland and from the memories of a childhood she didn't want to remember. Three riders abreast, one leading her mount, trotted closer. Scouts, of course, come to see if she'd done her job.

"Ho," She called out, and the rider leading her stallion dropped the reins. The horse picked up speed and cleared the distance to her in the time it took for her to take two steps toward him. She reached out for his nose so she could feel the wet. She was starved for fluid, to feel it on her skin, in her lungs. It felt good to have the snot and sweat against her palm. It felt real and grounding. Reins slapped against her other hand as he nuzzled against her, and with a deft movement she had looped them around her wrist so he would stay close.

Without looking at the other rider as he trotted closer, she reached into her saddle bag to feel for her tunic. She knew it was still there. It was a leather thing with sewn-in chips of garnet, a garment lovingly sun-bleached by her nurse so many years ago in anticipation of her wedding. Now, just over a decade later, it was the only thing left that would fit her, and she'd worn it so long nearly all the chips of garnet had long disappeared and the calf suede had softened even more to a nearly decadent linen feel against her skin. Even so, it was also grimy with her sweat. It had been a long trek finding these people.

She'd taken the tunic off, knowing the rain would come as she finished her task, making the leather difficult to wear in the torrent, later drying on her into a hard shell. She always took it off before battle then stood naked as she did her father's bidding, because it seemed the most respectful thing to do when you took the lives of others: to show your own vulnerability. Even so, for some reason this time, she was loath for the leader to see her undressed. He had a way of looking through her as though she didn't stand in front of him, but at the same time, of making her feel as though her nakedness was something abhorrent.

There were times she refused to get dressed just to make him pay for that look. She decided to leave her tunic where it was; he would never see her as a woman anyway. None of them ever did. Ever would. The other riders came up just as the clouds released the first drops of the surge. They kept their distance, but surveyed the battleground with some respect, if not deference.

She held tight to Barruch's rein and he sent a sulking pout her way, wanting his freedom; still, she didn't want to mount just yet. She needed to at least feel her feet on the ground when the rain came, wanted to feel it puddle upon, and then soak into, the gasping earth.

Drahl grunted and nodded at the prostrate form of a man a short distance away. "Was he the first?"

They rarely spoke to her, and she knew his question wasn't idle chitchat. He wanted to know if they'd charged her, if she'd slain them as they ran toward her, or if she'd gotten them from the back as they traveled unaware. Her father would want to know these things. He always wanted to know these things.

"He was the first," she said, and because she knew her father would want even more, added, "they didn't look as though they knew we were coming."

He nodded but didn't seem surprised.

She studied him. "But then, you knew that, didn't you?" She couldn't help the note of accusation she heard in her voice.

Instead of denying it or showing chagrin, he spat a thick globe of mucus that landed just next to his horse's hoof.

"It's not for a witch to question—only to serve."

She sucked in her bottom lip. Serve. Oh yes. She had served. She knew well her value to the tribe. She leveled him with a direct stare that she kept despite his narrowed gaze and threatening brow.

"I'm still thirsty," she told him and was rewarded with a quick, but just as quickly recovered expression of fear.

The sense of pleasure left when she saw it had been replaced with the usual loathing. No matter. She'd gotten as used to the hatred of her father's people as she'd grown of killing.

"Leave me while I collect the seeds," she said, waving him away. She knew this time there would be no herding of slaves; this time, like the last time, and the time before that, it was all about killing.

The rain had become a pelting blanket by now and she would need to collect the dried eyes so her father could count the number of vanquished before the rain washed them away and into the crevices of caked earth as it split apart from itself.

She flipped open the hemp sack hanging from the side of Barruch's saddle and pulled out a leather pouch to tie to the pommel, this she would use to dump in the dried raisins that had once been the fleshy, seeing eyes of the living.

Barruch had been with her long enough to follow without being led as she crossed the cracked earth. He'd grown with her and was the only present her father had ever given her. She'd been thrilled to find the midnight colored foal tied to a stake on her sixth season just outside her nurse's hut outside the confines of the village walls. She'd been less thrilled when she discovered it was only because her father had tired of taking her to war on the back of his horse.

Barruch had been with her when she'd deliberately killed her first man. And he gained a sort of language with her that was entirely delivered through his body language. During his first battle, he'd walked sideways away from each fallen man, trying to get away without actually retreating.

The first man from this battlefield lay face down, and she had to push him with her foot to roll him over. Barruch high stepped around him, showing a dainty disdain for death. Even in the flash of water coming down Alaysha could see the blackened bits of the dead's eyes lying an inch apart on the soil. For some reason, every eye her power contacted dried so badly it snapped from the brittle stems that were once connecting fibers. When she was little, she'd thought of them as the seeds of their souls and worried they'd fall into the cracks of earth she'd created, there to lay down roots as the rain engulfed and nurtured them.

At first, she worried about it enough she suffered terrifying night visions as she slept, but as the years passed and no newly sprouted man came to take his vengeance, she stopped worrying at all and began instead to pray for it.

Now, a dozen years past that time, she merely stooped to retrieve the seeds and tried not to look at the man when she rose to throw his eyes into the pouch. No use. Before she could amble on to the next, a dozen paces away, she had glanced down at the shriveled face and gaping mouth and the sight of it held her gaze captive for long, regretful moments.

She wished it didn't have to be like this.

Desiccated, a human looked like strangely tanned leather; this man was no different. He had a tattau beneath his right arm, that much she could tell; that alone made him different from any other man she'd killed. She paused to trace the line of inked-in soot stretching from tricep to hip in what appeared to be a perfectly straight line—or could have been perfectly straight if not tightened into a warped ribbon of ink.

The tattau made her fidget. She herself had a ribbon of ink stretched into a perfect line. Her's may have been stretched across her chin, but it was too much of a coincidence to ignore. She leaned in for closer study; it would be far too much coincidence if his tattau also showed stampings of skin through the ribbon, as hers did, mouthing flesh-words in a language she had never learned to decipher.

There, just discernible down the length of his ribcage were the symbols: not the exact same as her own, but similar enough that she knew the ribbon had been tattaued around open symbols. It was a strange mix, uncommon.

She looked up and scanned the grounds, letting the pools of rain drip down her bare shoulders. Through the cascade she saw a dozen other men lying at varying distances from her. She couldn't tell from her vantage point if they too were tattaued, but she could see they'd each been in various pursuits when she'd attacked them. Daily pursuits. Pursuits of regular living. One had a spilled basket of oval stones that had probably once been gathered eggs before she'd psyched the water from them; another lay next to a bundle of kindling, one clutched a spear, another a child. She squeezed her eyes shut at that one. The children always bothered her.

So. It was true, her belief that they had no idea they were about to face the Deities.

Past the dozen men who had been at toil when she'd arrived, sprawled now in unexpected death, squatted what she thought could be a dwelling. From her killing distance, she'd thought it was a hill; from this close, she could tell it had a maw of a door with desiccated thatch atop. A mud house, she thought, something that, in Sarum with its erections of stone and cement, she'd never seen but recognized from early childhood stories her nurse told of, while spinning sleeping tales about where she'd come from.

She lost herself in thought, trying vainly to catch the specter of memory and coax it into the light. What was it Nohma had said? It had something to do with those huts and these tattaus. Something about spirit fires and brown magic.

A crackle through dead brush startled her from her reverie, but she didn't need to turn around to know who it was. She could smell him; the red tobacco on his flesh, the musk of a dozen women, the sourness of a nursing babe that was his new favorite heir.

"It's you," she said and shifted so she could see him. She met her father's blue-eyed gaze with all the courage she could muster. He didn't usually come to witness her work, not since she had been very young and unreliable.

"I hadn't thought to see you, Father."

His gaze slid over her so quickly she doubted he saw her at all. It fell instead on the seeds nestled together in her palm.

"I come to see the battlefield, not to court a witch."

It stung. It always stung, that condescension. She should be used to it by now, but even eighteen years couldn't blunt the edge of that sword.

"A witch was useful enough for you on this battleground."

"Is there another use for a witch?"

She ignored the words. "Who were they, Father?"

He shrugged and rain ran off his shoulder to pool on the top of his boot.

"I see you've let the fluid return." He spread his arms to indicate the gathering storm.

It was her turn to shrug. "It always returns. It has nothing to do with me."

"So you always say." It was a simple statement, but it held a note of accusation. She knew he believed more of her.

Still, this was more than he'd spoken to her in a year and even though she hated herself for it, she pressed forward.

"This was no battlefield."

"A battlefield—a war—has many forms."

"And one of its forms is a peaceful village?"

He cocked his head as his gaze met hers, his hair so like his albino mount's mane, long and thick and tangled, plastered against his skull from the rain. He looked like a vulture then, with his great hooked nose and hooded brow. She should have seen the resemblance before. He was a bird of scavenge, not of prey.

"What were they to you, Father, these peaceful people?"

"Who said they were peaceful? And who said they were people? You know as well as any warrior, targets are things, not people." He turned on his heel in dismissal, kicked the hand of the prone corpse at her feet. "Now collect the seeds of yours and bring them for the count."

He took what she thought were deliberate steps toward his mount, but she caught him stealing a surreptitious glance at the horizon where the vultures were gathering, where the copse of trees was, where the fluid still rested in the fibers of each living thing there, and she saw him worry his bottom lip with his teeth.

And she wondered in that moment what might have Yuri, fierce Leader of a Thousand, Conqueror of Hordes, so concerned.

Chapter 2:

The village was a small, mobile one. If she could name it, she'd have to call it nomadic, except it showed signs of having recently put down roots, and didn't seem to show an inclination of movement for a while. She was right about the mud hut. No community of people would take the time to pile soil into one place and hollow it out and thatch the top just to move on when the food source had thinned. In full view, she could tell that great care had been put into its erection; it could have been perfectly oval with vertical slits for air.

Yet, there were signs of travel too: many dwellings were the stick and skin kind that allowed for easy tear down and set up. And these were scattered in what was once a grassy clearing at the opening mouth of a great forest.

It had taken her father's camp and riders five days from Sarum to find a site close enough to the coming battle she would only have one full day of riding to reach this village. They'd been on campaign for most of the season already, and had stopped in Sarum for a mere five days when his scouts returned. There had been a flurry of activity then; she'd seen it from Barruch's stall as she mucked it out and Barruch watched her with a sense of entitlement she'd come to expect from him. She'd known the men would be moving out again soon; she'd traveled much in her years as Tool to the Emir, and she recognized the appearance of an army about to pull out.

She knew this clearing too and she knew the woods beyond. Both were on the cusp of a great body of water stretching farther than she could see and larger than she

---

could drain. It was a smart place for an innocent village to lay down roots. A foolish spot for a target of annihilation to do so.

Alaysha had collected fifteen sets of eyes by the time she'd reached the hut: ten men, two children, and three women. One of the children had been an infant clutched in a woman's arms. She'd been pregnant, so she supposed she should increase the count to sixteen even though she'd have to explain to her father why she didn't have that many pairs of seeds.

The hut held another three; all settled around a fire pit still smoking from newly spent ashes. She stood next to the pit and peered up. Smoke puddled at the ceiling, trying to make its way out of the small hole left for ventilation so the inhabitants didn't have to worry about falling sick from inhaling smoke-filled air.

She was so weary; she felt like every emotion in her body was somehow trying to do the same thing as the smoke.

Alaysha found herself squatting next to one of the women hunched lifeless next to the fire pit. The old woman stared unseeing at her own eyes that had fallen to the ground in front of her. They were larger than the others she'd collected and were not nearly as shrivelled, but there they lay just the same. About an inch apart, but one slightly offside as if it had rolled after it had fallen.

She reached down to scoop them and said, as much to hear her own voice as to apologize for the disrespect of another, "Sorry, Mother." She palmed the two seeds and tightened her fist around them. "I need to take these from you." She had an insane urge to pat the old woman on the shoulder in condolence, but resisted. Once more she wondered why she had been sent to destroy these people.

The old woman kept her counsel as Alaysha expected, but there was a subtle shifting of the smoke so it seemed to collect itself from the ceiling and the air around her only to snake around the woman's throat. It was so subtle that at first Alaysha didn't realize anything had changed in the hut until she thought to recheck the ceiling and discovered it was clear. She knew then it was no ordinary smoke.

She fixed her attention again on the fire pit. Ashes, yes, and bits of blackened wood, but something else too. She closed her eyes and breathed in: frankincense, rosemary, sage. They could be merely for fragrance to rid the air of the stagnant musk of wet soil. Yes. Perhaps. She inhaled again, this time more deliberately, more focused. Concentrating. Another scent: an older one than mere herbs. The smell of souls roasting, she thought. Brimstone, then.

"Who were you, old crone," she said out loud. "That you could mask that stink?"

Better question might be why she would be burning brimstone in the first place.

She craned her neck, trying to peer under and up at the old woman's face. No eyes, of course; Alaysha had those in her hand. The cheeks were hollowed in from age as well as the leathering of the battle. The mouth hung open, jaws as unhinged as a serpent's, readying for a meal. The chin—

Alaysha scrambled to her feet so fast she fell on her backside twice before she found solid footing. By then, she'd backed into the wall and her palm had contacted the cracks of dry dirt. Her hand went through and half the wall released itself in a shower of earth. It caked at her feet as the rain streamed in and kissed her cheeks with wet.

"Who are you, old crone?"

She stumbled back to the fire pit, afraid the whole wall would cave in and with it the whole hut, and she'd be trapped there under the weight of dry soil getting ever heavier as the rain soaked it.

The old woman remained just as quiet as her death demanded, so too did her companions, both of them hunched forward, their hands stretched out before them on the ground, palms up, supplicating almost. Their eyes also awaited collection.

Alaysha had to steel herself to press closer and reach for the seeds. She had to force herself to peer under and up at their faces too.

Tattaus. Each one just like the first. Stretched in ribbons across their chins and into their hairline. Tattaus filled with symbols of flesh showing through, of an ancient language that seemed familiar but unlearned.

Tattaus even more like hers than the man outside.

She couldn't see the smoke anymore. It must have found its way out of the crumbling hole she'd made in the wall. She shook the seeds around in her palm, staring out the hole and watching the rain collect in the crevices made of the cracked earth. It puddled up through some, collected in holes and started to move like something alive. The gap itself started to melt and the wall to split farther. The torrent would collect in any riverbeds outside and sweep this village and its bodies into outlying areas, scatter everything until it was unrecognizable anymore. And this hut would collapse on her soon if she didn't get out.

Still, these women, these crones—elders they must be—had a secret she desperately wanted to know, and she wasn't leaving without at least one of them.

Without thinking of respect or propriety, she began yanking one by the arm, dragging her along the earth toward the door, and when the rain and dirt had mixed into a slick mud that stole her grip from the leathered arm, she grabbed a foot and buck-yanked until she managed to get the woman halfway through the opening.

Too late, the mud hut collapsed on itself, the weight of the rain turning the caked dirt into a muck that greedily held onto everything beneath it.

She fell backwards onto hard wet ground. It couldn't be. Not this close. Not this close. She'd nearly had her.

A sob got stuck somewhere between her chest and throat. She choked. Even as the torrent plastered her hair and made her limbs immobile from cold, she felt the hot tears mingle on her cheek.

She could have sat there for ten minutes or more, letting the rain course down over her chest, but the sense that she was completely nude and hip deep in a puddle of muddy water tempted her to stand. She swiped her eyes with the back of her forearm. She'd been foolish letting a few dead women bother her so. Hadn't she seen dead women plenty of times? Yes, she told herself—so much it should have made her complacent by now.

If it just hadn't been for those tattaus. That was the trouble. She hated crying, had learned to steel herself against the tears long ago, had learned to steel herself against almost every emotion that could bring the power, but these women, these markings—they discomforted her.

She sighed, frustrated at herself and the pile of mud that had buried all but the feet and shins of the crone. Maybe she'd return in a week when the water ran off and soaked in and dried up. Maybe she'd dig the women out.

For now she was spent. And wet. And cold. She whistled for Barruch and was surprised to hear him blowing air just on the other side of the hut. He clomped out from behind it and ambled over to her. He turned his head, finicky, to the side and showed her his jawline.

"You old fool," she whispered to him and he nickered in response. He was soaked and obviously unhappy as he wasn't one to wait in the open rain while she made her collections. He was either hauling her the length and breadth of the recovery grounds, or he waited patiently somewhere sheltered. This plain wasn't big enough for the first and it lacked the latter.

"It's okay," she told him. "It'll be over soon." She stared past the hut where the trees were. See?" she said. "The sun is shining over there."

He blew irritably, and she couldn't help chuckling. "I'd like to dry off too."

She'd rather a bath and a hot fire, but she knew the longing for those things was about more than just getting clean and warm, and that neither of them would ease her spirit the way she always hoped it would. A truly hot bath was a thing for Sarum, and Sarum was a long way away. There was nothing for it, she knew, so maybe today would be the day she didn't hurry back to that bath in her nearby stream and that fire stoked outside her camp, and later to that inevitable interrogation. Maybe today her father's inquisition could wait.

She flung herself onto Barruch's back, planning to lead him to the copse where she'd dismount and lie on the moss, let the sun warm her. Then she'd pull on her tunic and wait for the rain to stop if it hadn't by then. It had already slowed down enough she didn't have to continually squint against the raindrops to see.

"He'll send someone for me, but we won't care will we?" she said, patting her mount's neck as he plodded toward the copse. With each step, Barruch seemed to pick up his pace and she guessed he was tired of death and wanted to retreat somewhere where he didn't have to put up with it. For a warhorse, he certainly could be fastidious.

She was a few hundred paces out when the rain did stop; the sunshine was so bright on the tree stand ahead of her she had to shield her eyes. The sun felt good on her back. Maybe she'd dry off before she even got there and they could just take the time to relax instead. She already knew the spot where they'd stop. Right there, where the twinkling of sunlight reflected back at her.

Wait. That wasn't right. No light would be twinkling from a focused spot like that in the middle of trees—not even if it was reflecting off water. Not at that height.

"Something isn't right, Old Man." She squeezed Barruch's sides with her knees and he stopped. She studied the area a few seconds more, chewing her lip in thought.

"Best get ready," she told him and he snorted in reply, himself breathing in a large draft after as though he was about to launch himself and needed bracing.

She reached into her side bag and pulled out her tunic then, still seated, pulled it down over her head, stretching her arms into the sleeves. It might be nothing there in the shadow of the trees, but she'd rather face nothing dressed then face something unknown naked.

The leather stuck in places against her skin and she had to hold onto Barruch tighter with her knees so she could pluck the material away and smooth it down.

The light flashed again and disappeared, leaving just the lush greens of trees and vegetation. Right. She was glad she was dressed. She spurred Barruch into a gallop. He was so responsive to her after these years that he was off in seconds. If there was something there, she wasn't giving it time to escape. And she knew something was there. Someone. And someone being there meant at least one person had escaped. Or fled.

And the person was watching her.

She charged the tree stand, lying down against Barruch's back, hugging his neck, becoming part of the horseflesh, letting the scratch of brambles and tree branches caress her arms. There was so much noise from the horse's panting breath, from the sound of him pounding the ground that she'd never hear if someone slipped out through the brush. That didn't mean she was going to give them time anyway. She knew the exact spot where the light flashed, hadn't taken her eyes off it and she went for the stand with all her concentration.

It was a small clearing, big enough for a horse to stand and a young woman to jump down and peer, crouched, into the underbrush.

Nothing.

She should have known that as fast as Barruch could be, he'd never outrun a spy who was watching the approach in the first place. But she had hoped she could at least catch the person running off.

She stood up and scanned the area. She should be able to see where they'd gone. There was a patch of grass that was crushed, a broken tree branch, nothing else. So that was where they'd watched from. She stood in the middle and turned in the direction of the hut. Sure enough, she had a good enough view of what remained of it but nothing was overtly clear. Would the person have been able to make out facial features or count the dead at this distance? She tried. She knew exactly how many dead bodies there were, but at this distance, she couldn't really say she "knew" they were bodies—they just showed as smudges of black against the earth. She couldn't even see the feet she knew were stuck out from beneath the pile of mud.

Barruch neighed from behind her and pressed impatiently into the growth. She watched him peering from behind a few tree limbs he'd managed to hide in. She gave him a warning shush before she turned back to squint into the underbrush ahead of her. The tree limbs behind her made an annoyingly loud crackling sound.

He whinnied in protest.

She'd have to do some training with him on not being so sassy.

"Really, Barruch?" she said, turning to him.

There, not three feet away, stood a youth perhaps a year or two older than she, his leg lifted; ready to swing onto Barruch's back. Barruch was not being overly cooperative and had swung his hind quarters toward a tree so the man was having a hard time getting into place.

"Get away from my mount," she said.

Best to not to let her gaze travel to the sword hanging on Barruch's other side. She was well-trained with sword and knife, even long sticks, but she rarely used the broad steel attached to her saddle—why would she? The great Yuri's witch had no need of a sword to kill, but this boy—this man, actually now that she'd seen him well enough—would surely use it if he could.

"Get away from Barruch," she said again, setting the spring in her lower back just in case she had to lunge.

Instead of obeying, he yanked hard on the reins so Barruch had to move away from the tree. His forearm muscles tightened and with a quick sweep the man's leg was up and over, and adroitly turning Barruch's nose toward her. With one hand he held onto the reins, with the other, he reached out to her. His fingers were long and elegant but for the roughness.

"Get on," he said.

Get on? Oddest kidnap she'd heard of—not that she'd heard of many. Her mother had been the last, but she'd not even been born and had to hear it years later.

"No." She told him.

He shrugged, and flashed a dazzling grin. "You'll miss him."

She stood, letting the tension she'd loaded into her spine relax. "I will not; he won't go with you."

A chuckle then, and a coaxing cluck. Barruch started to move.

She forged forward. "Wait. Barruch. Kneel." It was all she could think of. She'd taught him the trick to go down onto his front legs long ago as a trick to please her father. It always meant a parsnip or two for the beast— something the horse loved more than a free run. It took a second, a heart stopping second when she thought he wouldn't obey, but then, down went one knee and with a laborious groan, down went the other.

She knew the rider would have tried in that second to dig in, so he wouldn't fall, but it wasn't nearly enough time and he pitched forward instead, landing on his side in the grass. Alaysha took the time he was recovering to dash forward and wrestle her sword from Barruch's side. With it, she stood, feet braced apart, sword raised to her right with both hands on the hilt. He'd think twice if he meant to capture her. Or take her horse.

"I wasn't trying to steal him." He hoisted himself to his elbows.

"No?"

"No. Or steal you if that's what you think."

"You couldn't anyway."

"Oh, I see that."

"What do you want?"

He looked her over, his glance lingering a little too long on her chest. She had the horrible feeling that he'd seen her naked as she'd done her father's bidding, while he hid in the trees. He couldn't possibly have seen any real details from this far out, but somehow, she felt as though with him, it was possible. Her neck burned and she had to fight the urge to lower her gaze in shame. Instead, she shifted the blade so it was to her left. Just enough to make a motion to distract him.

"You didn't tell me what you're after. Why are you here?"

He put an innocent hand to his bare chest. "Me? Why are you here?"

She didn't need to answer him; he'd undoubtedly seen everything—or at least enough to know her presence was not mere happenstance. She gave him a dry glare that prompted him to protest.

"Oh, that?" He waved his hand in the direction of the village. "I know all about it. I even know why."

"Then why ask?"

"Because I want to know why you think you're here."

She lifted her shoulder, more to ease the ache beneath its blade than anything else. "I know exactly why I'm here." In fact, she knew all too well. It wasn't a difficult concept, after all.

"Not here." He stamped his foot against the moss and spread his arms. "Here." He gave her an exasperated sigh when she didn't say anything. "You have no idea who you are."

"And you do?" She snorted.

He turned his attention to her sword and nodded at it. "Why don't you put that thing down? I think we both know you don't need it."

She lowered the blade, but let it rest against her thigh. It might be true she didn't need it, but he might, and she wasn't about to make it easy for him to take it from her.

"Good," he said. "Good. Now, come, let's sit."

He settled on his patch of grass, crossed his legs and patted the spot in front of him.

"As though we were old friends?" She gave his hand a wary glance.

"Certainly not," he agreed. "How can we be? I've only known you a few moments. Now your nohma—well, I knew her for a while longer."

Now she gave him an even warier glance. He couldn't possibly know her nohma. She'd been dead at least a dozen years. She met his gaze across the space, his eyes, this close, looked like amber. She'd always liked that stone. She thought she remembered her mother's eyes when she looked into his. For a second she was flustered, then she remembered what he'd said.

"You're lying."

He spread his arms, a gesture of abject innocence, one that made him look even younger than she thought he could be. "Why would I lie?"

She didn't know, but she wasn't foolish enough to say so. Instead she took her time to look him over and she made no attempt to conceal the scrutiny. Let him know she was searching for weakness or ferreting out falsehood. Let him feel nervous.

What she got for her effort was a brush of fingers through his black hair. It wasn't as short as she'd thought at first—rather it was tied back at some point with a leather thong and had come mostly out of its queue, and was hanging over his ears but stopping short at his chin. His wide set eyes watched her watching him, and he leaned back almost arrogantly onto one palm, thrust his chest forward, giving her good study. She could make out markings beneath his arm running vertically down his rib cage.

"Who are you?" She did her best not to stare at the tattaus.

"Someone who knows your nohma obviously."

"You don't know her." Now she had him—anyone who really was telling the truth would not use the present tense.

"I do," he said."

She shuffled her feet, gave them great consideration. "Good ploy."

"How could I be making a ploy?"

"Everyone has a nohma, and so it would be easy to say you knew mine, hoping you would fool me into thinking you do know her."

He chuckled and placed his palms behind his head, leaning back farther against a tree.

"Stop it," she said.

"Stop what?"

"Acting unafraid. Acting as though you have nothing to fear from me." She wasn't sure why, but this bothered her.

"Okay." He sobered and sat at attention. So intent was his amber gaze on hers, so familiar, she had to turn away to avoid the intensity, and the sense of pull it had on her.

She hoisted her sword and slid it back into its sheath on Barruch's sidesaddle, then hoisted her leg onto his back. She didn't care who he was anymore; he wasn't trying to kill her, and if he'd escaped her "mission" so be it. Let him escape.

She was nudging Barruch forward when he spoke again, but it was too late. She was already heading out of

---

the grove, and once her mount had his mind set, she knew there was no changing it.

"It's not everyone who calls her nurse Nohma, though," he said to her back.

Nohma. Grandmother. He was right. She called her nurse something her father's tribe did not use, and so it was possible he did know her—but for the small fact that her nohma was dead. That was how she knew this man was just aiming his arrows into the shadows, hoping to hit a target.

Nohma was dead. Never mind his present tense. She was gone. Alaysha knew it was true because she was the one who had killed her.

Chapter 3

As it turned out, she left at just the right time. She could see both Drahl on his black mount and her father on his sturdy white one off in the distance, heading toward the decimated village. Looking for her, she supposed, but not from concern. If her father was riding with Drahl it could only be because he'd grown tired of waiting for a report; he hated waiting.

She trotted Barruch to meet him. They didn't see her at first; they kept on such a straight trajectory for the village, and by the time she'd started riding, they were already a breath ahead of her. She came up from behind them and to their left.

"Ho," she hollered.

They reined up short. The village ruin was a few hundred mount strides off yet, but she could easily make out the rubble of the old mud hut. She shifted her gaze away from it and made for her father's horse.

"I have the collection, Father," she told him and lowered her glance to his horse's hooves. No one could keep the intensity of his blue-eyed gaze long—least of all the witch he hated.

His horse snorted as it was forced closer, he and Barruch had been sired by the same stallion and though the speed ran in their veins, so too did the alpha streak. These two horses could not be corralled together and this proximity made them both antsy. Barruch was wont to nip at his brother, and stomp on a stray foot with his. Adding to that fact, it sensed the danger that Alaysha could drain the beast of all fluid. Add also the tension the beast felt from her father's very real, but checked, hostility. The cipher made for dangerous territory.

Yuri reached across both mounts, stretching toward the pouch. "How many?"

She unleashed the sack from Barruch's saddle and pulled out the pouch, handed it by its lashings to her father. "Eighteen pairs."

Yuri's fair face flushed red. "Eighteen?" He grabbed the handle and twisted to shake it at Drahl. "Eighteen pairs."

Drahl hung his head but said nothing. Alaysha wasn't sure what the trouble was.

"I collected them all, Father. Even the children's."

He didn't sound as though he believed her. "All, you say." He opened the top and rooted around within as though he could tell one shriveled eye from another, as though the contents weren't thirty-six eyes at all, but a benign collection of baubles. "All, you say." He withdrew his hand and yanked the pouch closed, then tossed it to Drahl.

"Tell her, Drahl."

"There were to be nineteen dead."

"Nineteen," Her father repeated. "Now tell me, where is the last?"

She swallowed hard. "The last?"

"You counted eighteen and there were to be nineteen. Where is the last?" He enunciated very clearly, very slowly, almost as though he thought she was stupid. But she wasn't stupid. Anxious, maybe. But not stupid.

"One woman was with child, but eighteen is all I killed, Father."

"Don't call me that," he said so matter-of-factly she wasn't aware of the venom in his tone at first. "I may have stolen your mother for my pleasure, but that doesn't make me your father. It makes me your Emir."

"Yes, Fa… yes, Yuri, Conqueror of the Hordes." Best to use his formal name, the one he prided himself on.

"It makes you my tool."

She nodded. She wouldn't react. He was angry, that was all. He always got this way when he was angry. Always trying to hurt her, to goad her. To test her. She would not react.

"Yes, Yuri."

"Where is the nineteenth?"

She wouldn't look at him. He would know if she showed him her eyes. "I killed only eighteen." It was true, wasn't it? He couldn't accuse her of lying.

He swore and pressed his mount closer. Barruch grew agitated. He stomped and writhed under her hold.

"I know you killed eighteen," Yuri said. "For if you had killed one more, I would have nineteen sets of your seeds."

He pressed so close Alaysha could smell the onions on his breath, the cactus wine he drank before each battle. She had to work to keep Barruch from rearing.

He pressed his spur into her bare shin and twisted. She gasped.

"There is no nineteen."

He glared at her, his blue eyes like chunks of hail and for a second she thought she'd like to melt the ice, drain it from him, taste the wet—

"Don't even think it, witch," her father said and she lost the thirst so fast she could taste the desert on her tongue.

"I'm sorry, Father."

He let the title slide, but he seemed to be considering it. Finally, he addressed Drahl, who had dismounted and was standing with his feet apart, the leather riding breeks buckled at the knees.

"Your scouts were wrong."

"I scouted the village myself."

"Then you were wrong."

Drahl kept the flint of his eyes cast downward and his thick lips pressed firmly together, but his posture argued with Yuri in ways his words would never dare. He opened his mouth once and then clamped it shut, considering. Then, he changed tack. "Perhaps the nineteenth was away during the attack."

Yuri rubbed his broad thigh in thought. "Perhaps," he said after a while. "Then we need to find out who was missing." He glanced at the basket of seeds. "That will be useless."

He turned Alaysha. "What of the bodies?"

She relayed what she could remember, leaving out the information of the tattaus and the man in the oasis.

"Three crones you say?" His face lit up at the news. "Three?" He repeated, holding up his fingers. "You're sure?"

She nodded.

It seemed as though his joy was temporary if not tentative, as though he felt relief, but it was combined with wariness.

"And were these crones marked?"

She had to be careful; too much information and he would know she suspected something, too little and he would know she was lying. "There were some markings on the men, Father, but they meant nothing to me."

He wasn't mollified. "What kind of markings were they?"

He was baiting her, she knew. She wasn't sure why. She sensed he knew exactly how the tattaus looked, that they were very close to her own, but she wasn't sure if he understood just how similar they were. She guessed, and made a stab he'd gotten reports but had not actually seen the tattaus. She hoped as she spoke that he couldn't hear the tremble in her voice.

"They were symbols of animals. All across the chest and the backs of the hands." He'd know she was lying if he went to look at the bodies, and she prayed to the Deities he wouldn't. She wasn't sure why she had lied so blatantly when she could be checked up on so easily.

He eyed her critically. "And the crones?"

"The crones had no markings."

"None?"

She shook her head.

Yuri turned to Drahl. "You told me—"

Drahl shrugged as it became obvious to Alaysha that while he'd had been the one sent to do the scouting, he'd sent someone else and so now he couldn't speculate. Thank the Deities for his laziness.

"Markings are markings," he said and nodded at Alaysha. "How would she know what to look for?" The black look he gave her would have shriveled an apple.

"She tells me what she sees."

"Perhaps it is not the crones she saw."

"Perhaps not, but then the number would be wrong." Her father was beginning to lose patience, she could tell; his white brows were furrowed and meeting together over the blue-pink of his eyes. Drahl on the other hand, seemed oblivious.

"The count was correct." He argued. He hoisted himself back onto his mount and spent considerable time wrapping the end of the rein over his fleshy wrist. Alaysha thought he would grow fat when he stopped riding and scouting.

Yuri's eyes narrowed. "Then you have the wrong tribe."

"The crones must have escaped."

"If it's so and it is the correct tribe minus the old women, then the number would be sixteen. If it's the right tribe as you say, and the crones are the right ones, then the number would be nineteen. Either you are right or you are wrong."

It was all terribly confusing. Alaysha cut in. "The crones did not escape."

"But they have no markings."

"They were the only old women in the village."

Yuri dismounted and grabbed the pouch again, then spilled the seeds across the caked dirt. Pick them out," he ordered.

Alaysha knew which were the crones. Each seed had its shape even if that shape was no longer what it had been when it was fully fluid, or if each seed lacked the color it wore in life. A witch does not send her power through tear ducts and pores and not know each fluid membrane it touches. By her very nature, she had a long, long memory, the better to travel the fluid lines of each host and drain the living fluid away. She knew each seed, yes. Intimately.

She sorted out seeds that in life she knew had been bright blue and milky white. Each crone with a mixed set. These not quite so desiccated as the others.

"These," she said, putting them aside from the others.

Yuri inspected them. "And all are buried beneath the mud?"

She nodded.

"And none were marked?"

It was her turn to examine the seeds, but only so she could avoid his eye. "Yes," she said, and found the lie came easier each time she spoke it.

He toed the dirt, flipping dry soil over the seeds. Then he said to Drahl, "It's not the right tribe. Keep looking."

"But the number is right."

Yuri didn't raise his voice, but the threat was clear in the undertones. "The number is wrong. There were eighteen, not the nineteen we're looking for. You counted wrong. The crones were unmarked. It doesn't matter if the others were. Keep looking."

Despite the way Drahl glowered at her and clenched his fat lips into a tight hateful line, Alaysha had to know. "Who are these people, Father?"

He stared at her. "The wrong people." He mounted up and nosed his stallion back towards the camp. Drahl did the same, leaving Alaysha alone.

The wrong people. He thought she'd got it wrong, but she hadn't, and now she needed to know exactly what was going on.

He wanted this village in particular vanquished. That was nothing new, not really, except for the crones. He was specific in asking about the markings too. Tattaus just like hers. But why? What had these people done that set him out from his beloved Sarum hunting for them?

She knew of at least one person besides her father who could answer that.

Number nineteen.

Chapter 4

Number nineteen was gone by the time Alaysha had returned to the tree line, and in spite of his having wanted her to accompany him, he'd undoubtedly left as soon as he'd seen the mighty Yuri and Drahl ride up to her.

It was the smart thing for him to do, no doubt, but the most frustrating for her. Now she'd never know what he wanted to tell her, and she had the feeling it was the same thing her father didn't want her to know. That meant she could never tell him the crones were actually the ones he was seeking. If the village had been the right one, he'd know number nineteen had escaped. Better he think they had the wrong village and that the survivor was nowhere in the vicinity.

It had been a terribly long day. She was hungry and tired, and worst of all, thirsty. That was never a good thing, but so long as she wasn't afraid, and she was sufficiently exhausted, the power could not creep on her unawares.

So she headed back to camp only to find that same camp being packed up. It was so like her father to break for Sarum without wondering if she had made it back safely or not. She knew the way of things. News just traveled. Drahl would have been given command to break and he would set his men about the task. The sundry womenfolk: laundresses and cooks, the children who cared for the horses and beasts, the hunters and gatherers, all would see the camp going through the motions of packing and would do the same without question.

She dismounted and led Barruch to her own encampment, a cleft of a cave in the side of a mountain about a hundred paces from the actual camp. Yuri's daughter or no, he never allowed her too close to his site. Too dangerous, he'd said. Drahl had merely told her no one wanted to be in close quarters with a witch.

She found it odd her father had been the one to soften the blow of that news.

She had meager belongings to collect: a bowl and a spoon, a bed blanket made of leopard fur and a thatch mat her nohma had woven years earlier with bits of feathers amidst the thatch to soften the grass. It rolled neatly and tied to Barruch easily.

She grabbed her bowl and spoon with the intention of scavenging a few morsels to fill her belly if the cook hadn't finished packing, then she'd take a few minutes to get some water from the stream next to the camp. She would rather the order be switched, but the stream would always be there waiting, while she had her doubts about the cook and his fare.

"Wait here," she told Barruch and gave his rump a pat. "If I'm lucky, there'll be a stray parsnip in it for you."

She left him peering down at the sour grass with disdain, and set out towards the cook's tent, trying not to meet anyone's eye. She needn't worry; most scurried out of her path as she approached.

Once or twice, when she encountered one of Drahl's men, they spat on the ground when she came near enough.

"Drink that, witch," one said, leering and poking at his friend's side.

"Watch it now," his companion said. "She can have you in one swallow."

"Brah," The first muttered, raking her with his gaze. "She's drank already. Killed a hundred men today already and half a dozen babies. Even a water witch can't drink more'n that."

Drink. They really had no idea. The man had been a soldier for as long as she'd been alive, and he'd seen the end of a dozen of her "battles", but he had no idea, still, what it was she did for her father. No one did. And so they assumed she put her lips to another's and drank their liquid away.

Fools. They thought they were safe if she didn't touch them. No one considered how difficult it would be to have to kill one by one and still be successful. Drahl might have had an inkling of what she did; he came upon her first deaths so quickly after battle, knew she hadn't a mark on her, knew she was too far away to touch anyone who died. He might have an inkling, and he might hate her out of fear, but he didn't really know the scope of her power. Most who had seen it used, had died within moments of witnessing it.

Only her father knew the full truth of it—had used her truth since she was old enough to be carried in a basket on his mount's sidesaddle. Had used her for his gain these last eighteen years.

Maybe it was a mercy they had no idea she could drain them even from this distance. And that was the fear of it—she could drain so easily—too easily, but she couldn't control it. Everyone, everything, every drop of water would obey her and gather for her, and move for her to the heavens until the weight of itself needed to be released: rain, hail, once even snow.

And afterwards she would be as thirsty as if she had been drained herself. So she could command the water, but it weakened her. And the more the power grew, the more it drained her when she used it. She'd been much weaker today after battle than she'd been during the last, over six months earlier. It wasn't enough yet to make her sick or helpless, but how long would it be before she collapsed after battle? How long before she fainted dead away?

And that was the secret her father could never know. He thought the draining empowered her, he thought the power came from the thirst.

She intended he always believe it.

Cook was all packed up when she neared his tent. His was the largest in the retinue but for her father's because of all the provisions he was in charge of and how many people milled about throughout the day. At the moment, no one sat near the now-dying fire or queued up for hot acorn mash tea. The old scent of roasted boar hung in the air, mingled with wild onions and the sweet fragrance of honeyed ale from last night's supper.

She knew the smell, sure enough, but she'd not been given a taste of the warrior's meal. She'd had to forage for her own acorns and dig a few wild onions and fern tops to steam over a lonely fire. She'd had no meat.

Cook caught a glance of her as she lurked close to the fire pit, scouring the rocks for stray bits of meat or vegetables. He had the decency, at least, to back away even though he lifted a pot at her—his way of fending her off, she supposed.

"I'm just looking for leftovers," she told him.

"There is none." Cook busied himself with rooting in a rucksack, stashing wooden utensils and tying up the leather thongs at the top. He was trying to avoid meeting her eye, she realized.

Alaysha noticed on the fringe of his stockpile a wooden plate with a short stack of griddle cakes and a few slices of burnt meat: bacon left over the spit too long, she figured, and no one had been interested in charred boar.

"What about that?" She pointed, and he followed her direction.

"That? That's rot, you fool."

"It looks edible enough."

He shrugged. "If you've a mind to eat burnt food, it's no care of mine. Save me from burying it."

Alaysha was headed to salvage the leftovers when a small girl bolted out from behind a stand of brush and made a grab for the griddle cakes with one hand and the bacon with the other.

Far be it for Alaysha to let a girl starve, but she was pretty hungry herself. She took after the scamp, hearing the unmistakable sounds of Cook chortling.

"Come back here," she yelled, trailing the girl past the brush and into the woods. "That's my breakfast."

The girl was fast the way a ferret is fast—she slunk through tiny gaps in trees, over the roots creeping along the forest floor, underneath the lowest hanging branches. She would have outdistanced Alaysha if she hadn't come up against the same hillside that had provided Alaysha a small cleft of sanctuary while they'd been out here.

She drew up to within a few feet of the girl and stopped, panting, as she decided what to do with her.

"That's mine," she decided on.

Up close, the girl looked even grubbier than she'd first seemed. Her long face had a gaunt, underfed appearance, and the smudges beneath her haunted eyes were black as the soot from the fire. The strings of her hair hung down in pigtails held together by mud—no lashing anywhere in sight. It was impossible to tell what color the tresses were through the dirt.

"Mine," Alaysha said again. She didn't care how starved looking this girl was, that food was well-earned spoils of war—her spoils—and she wasn't giving them up.

The girl was panting hard and her gaze never rested in one spot. It seemed as fidgety as a cornered ferret.

"Give it to me."

The girl shook her head and darted to the left, where Alaysha realized she'd tethered Barruch. They both started off at the same time, but Alaysha knew the girl would fetch up into a very large, very hungry, and very annoyed stallion. Sure enough, the sight of the black beast gave the child enough startled pause that Alaysha was able to make a grab for the girl's tunic—or what ragged pieces made up her tunic.

She gripped the edge of the coarse flax-spun as tightly as she could and simultaneously pressed the girl closer to Barruch.

"Give me my supper."

"I thought it was your breakfast," the girl taunted.

"It's both of those things."

The little ferret took one long look at the food still clenched in her hands.

"It's mine," Alaysha whispered, thinking the soft tone might soothe the savage expression on the child's face. "Please." She took hold of the girl's elbow, more to implore her than to hurt her.

And she was rewarded with teeth crunching into her tricep.

"Why you little—"

There was a flash of a dirty smile before the girl crammed the griddlecake into her mouth. Alaysha had to wrestle the bacon from her other hand even as the ferret chomped and swallowed convulsively, frantically. The girl's mouth and throat worked so hard, it was almost a thing of beauty—until, still fighting for the bacon, the girl started to choke.

"The Deities have mercy," Alaysha sputtered, watching the girl's eyes widen.

Instinct made the girl drop the bacon in favour of flailing at her throat.

Faced with a dying child or grabbing for a burnt piece of bacon, Alaysha let go the girl's tunic and made to help dislodge the stuffing of griddlecake that still puffed out the young cheeks and was obviously stuck in her throat.

"Maybe some water—" she started to say, and was frantically searching for a cup to dip some, when the girl whooped triumphantly, grabbed for the bacon, and in a flash tumbled under Barruch's belly and rolled to her feet on the other side.

Just like that, the little ferret was gone.

Chapter 5

The bats came while she slept under the stars. Alaysha could hear their clicking noises as they navigated in the dark, foraging for gnats and mosquitos. She rolled over on her thatch mat, curled into a ball and shivered. Sometime between her lying down and now, the temperature had dropped, and she hadn't thought to pull a skin over herself before dropping off into the land of shadows.

It had been one long, incredibly long and exhausting day. And the battle—she couldn't call what she'd done to that tribe battle—best she call it what it was—assassination. Yes, after the assassination and the search and the subsequent fight over her supper, she'd been so fatigued when the camp set back on their way to Sarum that she'd fallen asleep on Barruch's back at least three times. When the queue of riders stopped for the night, she hadn't even bothered to find a decent shelter, just unrolled her mat a few sans-kubits from the rest of the camp and fell onto it.

She could see the fire pit from where she sat now, hear Barruch's heavy breaths, feel the heat coming off his flanks as he stood close. She could tell he was sleeping even though he rarely rested for more than a couple of hours. Today must have been equally as tiring for him with all the travel. She'd have to make sure to see the wrangler for oats in the morning to help him build his strength back. He was no friend of Alaysha's but he hated to see a mount suffer. For now she should try to find a skin in her pack. Maybe with warmth, she could sleep 'til morning.

She rubbed her bare arms, hoping to stimulate the circulation and bring a flush of heat to the skin. She got up and leaned against Barruch as she rooted in the pack beneath him. He woke when she touched it and glared at her through unblinking lids. He snorted and moved a step to his left. She had to dig deeper.

Strange; the pack felt empty. No spoon. No bowl. And most definitely, no furred skin.

Someone had undoubtedly stolen the few possessions she owned, and there was only one person she could think of worse off than the water witch. No doubt the little ferret was cozied up somewhere wrapped in the fur and clenching the spoon with hope morning would bring a few meager crumbs to fill the bowl.

Alaysha sighed heavily. It would be a long wait 'til morning. She'd either have to build a fire in the dark without her tinder bundle, or brave the fire in the middle of the camp and its few sentries who kept it fed through the night.

She didn't relish the thought, but she patted Barruch's rump anyway. "Go back to sleep, old man," she whispered and he sent a cloud of hot air in response.

Barefoot, she made her way toward the fire pit in the center of camp. She stumbled a few times on tree roots, and got a twig jammed between her toes, but she knew the shrubbery of the camp fringes would eventually give way to the even, open plain of the main camp, and the going would be easier. She was intent on staring at the ground, trying to discern the way of it when she felt a dry palm clamp over her mouth.

She was already struggling and fighting into the palm bed when a second arm went around her waist and pulled her hard into a muscled torso.

Instinct told her to thirst, and panic came with it, like a hard hit to the stomach. If she drew the water, it would come from everywhere—including the camp. She could already taste the moisture and moldy scent of wet earth. The fear of that made the psyching of the water even stronger.

"Think of your nohma." The command was a hoarse but firm whisper in her ear.

Even though she was pinioned in strange arms, Alaysha was so desperate to keep the power from thirsting the camp dry, she deliberately went still. Through the trees she could see the fire flicker and then blaze higher as whatever water still remaining in the wood hissed into the air. Somewhere, she knew a laundress's linens, hung on outstretched tree limbs, had dried so completely they took the shape of the branches and would be stiff when lifted off and inspected in the morning.

Then, sweet merciful Deities, there was Nohma: her hair hanging in two plaits on her shoulders; blonde, with streaks of white; her hands working Kasha dough into thin pancakes to stretch across the fire. It was such an ordinary image, and yet such a sweet one that Alaysha held onto it.

The taste of leaf mold disappeared and the hiss of water through living wood evaporated into silence. It was all so sudden, she nearly collapsed into the arms of her captor. Never before had she been able to stem the tide of power. It always took flight from her so quickly, did its work so fast, it was impossible to recall before it killed.

She felt the relief, too, in the body of her assailant. His torso melded into her back.

"It's gone," he said to the dark. And because she couldn't speak she nodded.

"I'm going to take my hand away."

She knew the voice now. Number nineteen. He must have followed her to the camp.

"All right," he sounded unsure; she could still feel his body against hers, rigid, braced. She waited until she felt him relax before she eased out of his grip. He let her go in measures: first her mouth, then her waist. She spun around in the darkness, her hands outstretched, aiming for his throat.

There was no connection; just a band of thickened air meeting her grasp, and an amused chuckle in the dark.

"You really are young," he said. "Come with me."

He didn't wait for an answer. She felt him move away from her, heading back in the direction of her site. There was no waiting for her assent or her decision, and she knew she could easily make a break toward the fire and notify the sentries, shout, anything, and he must've known that too. Yet when she caught a glimpse of his back, it was already a good distance away, absorbing errant moonlight, and then it was swallowed by the shadows of trees and shrubs. She watched the blackness for some time before she followed, picking her way through the brush, wincing when she stuck the same toe as before on a rock she didn't see.

He was hunched over the beginnings of a fire when she made it back to her own site. She could just make out her tinder bundle as it rested on his lap, lit by the long, narrow light of a kindled flame. So it hadn't been the ferret after all who'd stolen her things. She wondered how long he'd lurked in the dark, waiting for her to sleep so he could ease the items from her pack. This thievery must have been what woke her, not the cold.

"Why didn't you just tie me up while I slept?"

He ignored the question in favor of blowing air onto the meager flame. It was being stubborn and seemed reluctant to catch. He mumbled a few foreign words at it and pulled the furred skin—her stolen skin—over his shoulders.

"Come," he said.

"You didn't answer me."

"I will, but first you need to sit with me under this fur."

She crossed her arms over her chest and edged closer to Barruch, who shambled nervously in the dark.

"Listen, it's only because you're cold," he said. "And so am I. Besides, if we are both under this, no one in the distance will think there is more than one of us here in the dark, even when the fire catches."

She turned her attention to the stubborn few tendrils of blaze teasing the few bits of wet sticks he'd piled together.

"It won't catch."

"It will."

"It won't last."

"It will last as long as we need it to."

"You sound certain."

"I am. Now, hurry up."

She wanted the heat, it was true. And she wanted more: the answers she hadn't been able to get from her father after the battle. And if she waited too long, someone just might take notice that the water witch had company— and such an oddity would undoubtedly draw attention.

She ran a palm over Barruch's neck and down his side. "All right," she said and made herself take the steps toward her mat and the hunkered-down form on it before she could change her mind.

Her visitor stretched his arms wide so the fur opened up, and she scooted beneath, between his knees, letting go a murmur of pleasure when the fur settled around her shoulders and the heat enveloped her.

"Better?" he asked, his breath against her nape.

"Better."

It was then the fire caught and she felt a flush of warmth on her cheeks.

"So, you followed me," she said, low enough that past their fire, no one would hear her speak.

"I did."

"How could I not have seen you?"

He chuckled, but said nothing.

"You won't tell me."

"I would be a fool to tell secrets to the enemy."

"And yet you cuddle beneath the furs with her as though you were a favored companion."

"You call this a cuddle, this shivering beneath a ragged skin with barely enough fur to hold the heat? You are indeed young."

She didn't like the way he said it. If he'd known how she'd lived these years, how many lives she'd taken, he'd not think her young. She was wise beyond most warriors' years.

"So it's true; we are enemies? It was you my father was searching for?"

"Yes. Me and the others."

"You mean the rest of the village."

"The rest of my tribe."

"So he's done it, then. Conquered your people?"

"Mere conquest is not what the great Yuri is after."

"What, then? What is he after if not the vanquishment of another tribe, the obedience of another horde to keep his boundaries safe?"

His tone turned chiding. "Is that what you think you're doing for him? Keeping his tribe safe?"

"I hadn't thought about it."

"And my enemy, who never once thinks about what she's doing, is expecting answers?"

"You came to me, not the other way around."

"Fair enough."

"So what is my father after, if not conquest?"

"Annihilation. And he very nearly has it. There are only two left from my tribe."

It hit hard, this news that she had decimated almost an entire group of people. She thought of the last battles—no, not battles if she remembered correctly—more plain murder. Yes, some of the first ones, months and seasons ago had been truer battles than these last, with men coming at her with swords and axes and arrows, while the villages they fought for waited hundreds of leagues away. But these last few had been less so, surprise attacks, even. She thought they were punishments or strategic blows. She'd never given thought to how many might be left.

"We've been travelling," she thought out loud. "Going far and wide to hit the targets."

"Because we're nomadic," he said.

"We've gone into the mountains."

"Our winter home."

"We've killed on the plains."

She felt him shrug. "Summer. Spring."

"I thought he was extending his borders."

"He was getting rid of us, and now he has nearly succeeded."

"But why? What did you do? Yuri is a fierce man, but to decimate an entire tribe—he must have a reason."

"Fear."

"The great Yuri does not fear." She snorted and Barruch clomped closer, trying to nuzzle beneath the blanket to investigate her sounds of derision.

"Yuri had reason to fear when he first conquered one of our villages twenty seasons ago."

"You can't know that."

"Why not?"

"Because you aren't twenty seasons old. How do you know what occurs in battle seasons before your birth—even war stories are filled with lies."

He laughed but there was no mirth in it. "You who are so young school me on age."

There was no sound in the darkness for a while. The fire, despite its meager fuel, burned hot with a blaze that made Alaysha think it was fed from beneath, from an infinite supply of the black sludge that sometimes gurgled to the surface.

She felt the wetness of Barruch's nose as he shoved his muzzle into the mound of blankets. She reached out to touch him.

"It's okay, old man," she whispered. "Everything is fine." In fact she was getting hot beneath the fur, and despite the excitement of being awake, of being with number nineteen, of being on the cusp of knowing things she'd always wondered about, the heat was like a shaman's drug. She had to fight against it. She felt his chin on her shoulder, and they sat for long moments before he spoke again. She had to force her eyes to stay open.

"I was six seasons old when your father came to our summer village."

"Then you do remember."

She felt his shiver against her back. "Yes. I remember."

She thought for a moment, wondering if she should press for more or let him be. She settled for asking the question he had instigated but not pursued.

"So who is this other? This second to last person in your tribe?"

"Haven't you guessed?" He pulled the fur tighter around them both, his right palm resting on her left shoulder. "It's you."

Chapter 6

Alaysha woke only when she heard birdsong. She expected number nineteen to be long gone, but he was stretched on her mat beside her, curled beneath the fur so only the topmost part of his black hair was visible. She'd expected him to have slipped into the night as quietly as he'd arrived. She expected he'd delivered the news he was meant to, shocked her senseless, refused to say anymore until she wearied herself with protests and slept, finally, to the sound of frogs calling to each other in the trees, and then been off like a shadow disappearing with the sun.

But no. At the moment, he had his hot palm resting beneath her tunic on her bare stomach as though it belonged there.

Face burning, and the clutch of anxiety tightening her throat, she scrambled from beneath the warmth and onto her bare feet where the chill pinched at her skin. She stood looking down at him, arms crossed, thinking of his words from the night before, of his refusal to say more until she was ready to hear it. Ready. What did he think she was now if not prepared to hear the truth?

Young, he'd called her, and here he appeared to have come straight off the blade-sharp edge of new manhood. She'd dislodged the fur when she'd jumped up and now the side of his face was exposed to the newly rising sun. His lashes reminded her of the tendrils of old smoke that still wound about the fire, and his jaw had the same smudge of color. Asleep as he was, he had no arrogance, no sense of danger. She shouldn't have bolted like a hare.

"You didn't seem to mind my hand on you during the night," he said without opening his eyes. "Why run from it now?"

"I was cold last night, obviously."

He pulled the fur higher, covering his chin. "Cold. Right. Come back to the mat. I'm the one who's cold now."

She thought she could feel embarrassment flush her face straight down to her toenails.

"Shouldn't you be disappearing like you appeared?"

"Why should I? I have a lovely mat. A lovely mount to ride. A lovely..." he said no more, merely opened one eye and lifted his hand to thumb his jaw. "Let's just say I find it lovely here."

She threw a harassed glance over her shoulder. The camp would be roused soon, have a quick breakfast and then be back on the road for another day's journey. Three more before they reached Sarum. She intended the camp make it there without discovering she harbored the enemy.

"You have to leave."

"Why?"

"Isn't it obvious?"

"What's obvious is you favor Yuri to your own kin." He sat up and wrapped the fur around his knees.

"Yuri is my kin."

He snorted. "Yuri is your conqueror."

"He's my father."

"Is he?" The boulder shifted and poked at the embers of the fire. To her surprise, it leapt to attention.

"You know he's my father."

"A father is more than blood, Alaysha."

She squinted at him suspiciously. They hadn't addressed each other all night. "You know my name."

"Of course. Know thy enemy, my nohma used to say. Well, until you killed her." There was something in his face that made him look different, but then it was gone.

"I didn't—" she started to protest, but realized it was pointless. Of course she'd killed his nohma. She'd probably killed them all.

He grinned at her, and it was such a knowing, patronizing look, she had to stifle the urge to strike him.

"I'm hungry," is what she said instead and made to root out some early, unfolded fern tops and some grain heads for her breakfast. A dove egg or two wouldn't be bad either. She'd use the lovely fire he provided her with and roast them right in their shells. Never mind what happened to him. No doubt he'd get found while she was away and be taken for a thief and stoned right there.

She left him with a decided glare and shuffled off into the underbrush. He knew her name, knew she was part of his tribe, knew her father had ordered them killed...

She stopped short, a green fern clutched in her hand, ready to yield when the thought settled into her psyche like a rat bedding down for the day.

He knew she was part of his tribe. Oh, dear heaven. And Yuri knew it too. That was the secret her father kept. Yuri used her to annihilate everyone of her own tribe right down to the last man.

The realization made her straighten so fast, blackness threatened to overcome her. She felt dizzy. She'd systematically killed every one who had a connection to her. Ignorance was no excuse. She'd been bid to do so, and she'd killed without question.

All but for one. Number nineteen.

And number nineteen, who knew what she didn't, was even now lying exposed on her mat, exposed to view of the camp. If they found him, they would kill him.

She darted back, through bracken and crashing through spindly trees, back into the scented grass, and the light of her camp. She rushed, breathless, toward Barruch and shoved him aside as hard as she could so she could see her mat.

She should have known he'd be gone, but it still deflated her. The mat was rolled up and propped against a tree. The fur spread over a boulder.

The fire was blackened and dead.

She sighed.

"He said to tell you he's got a name—he isn't a number."

Alaysha whirled about to find the dirty little ferret standing with her hand against a tree, balancing on one leg uncertainly. Ready to take flight, she supposed.

She had to be careful.

"You spoke to him?"

The ferret nodded.

"Do you know who he is?"

A shake of the head, a short chew on the bottom lip.

Alaysha relaxed.

"Have you come to steal something else?"

The girl let down her foot, unshod, Alaysha could see. Just like her. She glanced down at her own feet— wiggled the toes.

"Have you eaten?" she asked the girl.

"No."

"Me, either. What say we try the camp this morning?"

The girl fidgeted. "I don't think I should."

Alaysha reached out her hand. "You must be hungry."

The girl bobbed her head in agreement. "But they won't like it."

"I know, but I'm too hungry to care."

They set out, the ferret close at Alaysha's heels but never quite abreast. Alaysha found she had to continually talk to her over her shoulder.

"Have you no family?"

The ferret nearly trod on her heel when Alaysha slowed her pace enough to hear the answer. "Careful," she told the girl.

There was a quick, furtive shake of the ferret's head, her muddied plaits leaving fresh trails of dirt on her tunic front. It made Alaysha wonder if the dirt was applied fresh each morning rather than just being the result of the girl's unwashed state.

"No relatives at all?"

Another shake. A few quick peeks over her shoulder and to the sides. "I had a brother once."

"Once?"

"Yes. A few months ago he left."

Alaysha thought it over for a second. There was something unsaid in the girl's tone. "Escaped, you mean."

The girl stopped a few paces away. She hung her head.

"You're one of the captives of year sixteen, aren't you?"

"Year fifteen by your timeline; we don't—we didn't—measure time the same way."

Alaysha nodded. "I don't imagine." She sidestepped to dodge the round of dogs loosed for their morning forage. The great Yuri never fed his warrior's dogs—only his own—and so each morning they were sent out to hunt for themselves. She watched them run through the bracken and disappear into the underbrush. Their being awake and loosed would mean the camp was up, awake, and setting about the packing routine, ready to travel.

"If you were captured during year fifteen, why are you free? Why aren't you serving in the scouts households?"

Alaysha remembered that campaign; or rather, she remembered the smell of death, the taste of the water she thirsted from every living thing within her killing zone. She thought of the pouch of seeds from that battle, lying nestled in a dirt hole at the back of her room beneath the ground in Sarum, covered over by thatch and then rocks on top of that. She never tried to remember much more than those things. Remembering the people the seeds belonged to was too painful. But that particular battle had been difficult. The village had sent out wave after wave of men, trying to wear her out little by little rather than sending them all at once. She'd had to send the power out over and over again.

"Are you listening?"

Alaysha's gaze refocused. She must have been lost in thought to have missed what the girl was saying. "I'm listening."

The girl shuffled her feet through the turf. "My master—the one who—the one who took us in after the conquest, he worked us hard." She fleeted a look into Alaysha's eyes, and there was a peculiar intelligence within, something pitiful to waste on manual labor, which is what all those from that campaign were used for: kitchen slaves, horse muckers, stone cutters.

"And?"

"Well we didn't mind hard work. Where I come from, labour is not a harsh thing, but it was the—master— of the house more than the needs." The girl let her gaze drop to her feet.

It took a moment to sink in, and the realization made Alaysha's stomach turn.

"You mean the master—"

The girl held up her hand as though she couldn't bear to hear the words.

"Oh, sweet Deities." Alaysha said. "Sweet Deities, you poor thing." She reached out to touch the girl's filthy plaits. "So you ran away. Are you all right? Do you need to see a medicine woman?"

The girl seemed confused. "I'm fine," she said. "Just hungry."

"But you said—"

"I said my brother couldn't take it anymore and we ran away."

"Your brother?" The mosaic was coming together a little tighter, and Alaysha couldn't say the picture was any prettier than what she'd originally thought.

The girl nodded. "At first we went together. But the master is on the trail a lot and we couldn't stay together without fear one of us would be found, and so then, the other. He left nearly a full season ago and told me to stay with the camp when it travels, on the fringes, stealing food, and then when we were back in Sarum, to stay close to his dog's quarters. I could get more scraps from them—you know the dogs are so well fed, they often have most of what's left."

"But how could he leave you like that?"

The girl glanced up sharply and the look she gave Alaysha sent a shiver down her spine. "He hasn't really left forever—he's coming back. And when he does it will be with an army."

Alaysha wanted to say something, but they'd reached the beginnings of the camp and a horrible keening wail had begun that replaced the shiver running down

Alaysha's spine with goose pimples. She darted to the left where a small animal skin tent had been erected amidst trees with long horizontal branches. One of the laundresses, obviously. There were always about half a dozen of them each time the camp struck out, always pitched their sites closest to the outer edge so the warriors could strip off their blood-soaked linen armor as soon as possible and leave it at those washes—then pick it up on the way to battle.

Since Alaysha had been going on conquest with her father, those laundresses had less blood-soaked linen and more sweaty tunics to clean. Still, they clung to the old ways with a tenacity borne of needfulness. Should they become extraneous, no doubt the great Yuri would find some other use for them—less favorable, if he found tasks at all. He had said more than once how he hated having to feed an army.

Still, the pile of rags the woman moaned over was so small, so insignificant, it made Alaysha wonder what could possibly be so horrible. It was then she saw the true shape of the rags. Formed around a tiny body. A little flax-spun cap atop its head.

She caught her breath and found she couldn't exhale. She should have known. She should have known she couldn't stop the power.

She cast harried glances around her. Laundry stiff as it hung from branches, stretched-out spruce roots forming a drying line. The ground beneath her feet was crackling moss—dried to straw. The woman herself was un-stooped with age, but her lips were dry and her weeping was horribly tearless.

Oh, sweet Deities. They would know. They would all know.

The strength nearly left her legs; she had to force herself to back up. She knocked into the little ferret.

"And what could they do about it if they did know?"

She hadn't expected the girl to speak. She looked down at her, trying to focus on her mouth. "What?" she asked her.

"I said what would they do?"

"You heard that?"

"I've ears, haven't I?"

"I thought I—"

"You thought you weren't speaking." The girl shrugged. "They'll have figured it out by now." She pointed to the water station where several warriors were tipping clay jugs over and over, finding only puddles of water within to slake their thirst.

"It's why they're afraid of you?"

Yes. It was why they were afraid. Still, this was the tribe that had brought her up. She couldn't stand to see the suffering. She had to do something. Surely she could bring rain. So what if she'd only killed a few and thirsted out only surface water. It wasn't right.

"I have to do something." As much as she wanted to go the other way, she forced her feet toward the laundresses and her dead baby. How old must it have been? Weeks, surely, it was so small.

She stepped close enough to stand over the woman who held the tiny corpse in her arms. Alaysha could tell it hadn't been dried out completely. The eyes were closed, but they were still round beneath the lids. The tiny hands hanging from the swaddling blanket were gray and lifeless, but not brown and leathered.

Maybe she hadn't thirsted the life from it; maybe she wasn't responsible for all of this.

The woman must have felt her presence. She glanced up, pain streaking her features. Within a flash that pain transformed to rage when she saw Alaysha standing there.

"You killed her." The lips, dry and crackled as they were, had a hard time forming the words, but the tone was unmistakable.

"I didn't mean—"

"What good can come from suffering a witch in camp, in the Emir's reach? Living in fear you'll lose control. Well, go on; drink me, too. Send me to my babe."

"I can't."

"You won't." The woman would have spit at her, Alaysha knew; if she could have gathered the fluid.

"You think I don't know you? You think I don't know what you are, about your kind?"

"My kind?"

The woman would say no more. She stared ahead for countless minutes and then went about moaning aloud again, rocking over the form she held. Her grief was so painful, so personal, Alaysha had to hug her stomach to keep from vomiting.

A dry hand took hers, and she looked down into a pair of muddy, concerned eyes.

"Come on," the girl said. "We have to leave her."

A tug, and then a deliberate pull so Alaysha's arm stretched up and out.

"We can't do anything for her," the girl said.

Breaking her fast didn't seem appropriate now. The two staggered to the camp, searching for, and finding subtle notices that the power had indeed begun its work.

Thankfully, however, there were no more deaths: only dry gazes from the tribe and desperate, futile searches for water. The ground was dry—no morning dew—but other than that, it was clear the camp had weathered the worst of the drought.

Alaysha was relieved until she caught sight of Drahl making a deliberate path toward her, his bear skin cloak sailing behind him from the force of his stride. She had a feeling her father's morning brew had been drunk of its liquid, leaving the bitter, psyche-strengthening dregs of herbs behind.

She reached out to grab the girl's hand but clutched at air instead. She wasn't gone exactly, just had wandered aimlessly toward a tent smelling of cinnamon and oats. Probably scouting for fare easier to get than Cook's stomach-fortifying roasted boar slabs.

Drahl stopped a few paces from her, staring sidelong at the woman still wailing over her baby. "The great Yuri, Conqueror of Hordes—"

"Leader of Thousands, yes, I know the title," Alaysha said, sighing. "What does he want?"

"He wants the witch to stand before him." Drahl wouldn't meet her eyes we spoke, but neither would he keep his attention on the mourner.

"Has it to do with a sudden lack of water?"

He did look at her then, and Alaysha could almost taste the spit he would have sent her way if he'd had enough available to do so.

"The witch should ask him," he said.

"The witch will."

His lips worked for a while before they settled into a hard line. Without another word, he turned his back and strode off. Alaysha didn't need to follow him—she knew exactly where her father's camp was even if she'd never been allowed within a hundred horse strides of it.

Her power must have done more damage than she'd thought. She tilted her head upward, to the gathering pinkness of the dawn sky. There were clouds just overhead, thickly white and clumped like clotted goat cream. Not enough water to make them heavy enough to let go, but enough to fatten them. She believed the pitiful stream they'd settled next to the night before was probably dry, and they'd have to journey nearly a day before there was another river large enough to fulfill all the needs of camp. Hopefully, there were a few pools along the way. The skins would need bloating if they were to make it home alive.

Chapter 7

Drahl left her a few paces from her father's site. It was pitched so his tent was backed into the side of a verdant hill, the more to shade him in the morning while he slept. On all other sides there were smaller tents where his guard intermittently kept watch and slept. His personal cook's tent, a short, flat-topped one made of bear skins, was in the middle of the area, a fire crackling merrily, its flames licking upwards to the rotisserie of sizzling hare. It would be cinnamoned and honeyed, that hare, its belly stuffed with wild apples and dried cranberries from the last season. Bodicca, a tall, wiry woman whose prowess as a warrior was only outmatched by her fame as a savoury cook, stood over the wrought iron, ladling herbed boar fat over the back of the meat.

Alaysha's stomach grumbled.

The woman glanced up sharply, and the circlet of men's teeth she'd stretched around her forearm jangled. Alaysha could make out the weathered look of skin needing fluid. Though the woman was watching her, Alaysha couldn't meet her eyes.

"My father asked for me."

Bodicca said nothing, just set the bowl of fat down and lifted a tankard to her lips, then made a great show of surprise before she upended it over the grass.

Nothing spilled out.

Alaysha wanted to say it was fortunate the food hadn't dried to leather, that it was lucky the honey she was using hadn't crystallized beyond use—that they were all damn lucky to still be alive. But those were all the reasons she'd been ordered here in the first place, and they all knew it—and feared it—and that fear brought anger, not relief. She had no choice but to keep her tongue, and instead settled down onto a log on the very edge of her father's camp, listening to the trembling song of the flute player rousing him to audience.

Her mouth watered at the aromas, but she did her best to seem unaffected while she waited. Under the circumstances, she'd rather not appear vulnerable in any way to her father. The piper's notes grew ever more grim, and Alaysha assumed the time for Yuri's appearance—and her own punishment—was drawing close.

She watched the cook pull out a hammered silver platter and lay the roasted hare on it, then circle it with roasted eggs. Usually they would be boiled, but not this day. She topped the eggs with roasted seeds and then set the plate down next to the tankard she'd upended earlier. It seemed the lack of liquid would be as much part of her father's repast as anything else—and intentionally so. All the better to make him angrier.

Well, his wrath wasn't quite so fearsome as all that. Alaysha would just have to prepare herself for the chastisement as best she could, and remind her father of the things she'd done for him. Certainly, she'd lied about the identity of the village she'd finished, and that meant they would be traveling and searching even longer for nothing, but it also meant he might feel some wariness, thinking those he was hunting were still out there somewhere. Until then, he needed his water witch.

She felt remarkably safe.

The tent flap was flung open and a slave held it aloft so the great Yuri could stretch before he fully exited; Alaysha could tell, even from her distance, he'd chosen to be bare chested, all the better to display the muscled arms and huge girth of his torso. He had his riding leggings on, the ones with sewn-in amethysts that protected him from dishonesty. Around his head, he wore the Circlet of Conquest—a self-designed, hammered-bronze line that had three jagged points on the front.

He was obviously dressed for intimidation.

He strode forth with a wave of his hand to Bodicca. She neither bowed, nor knelt. Not this mighty woman. She was as much a guard as any of the muscled men that shifted their way around camp. She cooked for Yuri because she wanted to, and because she'd earned his complete trust. She picked up the platter and passed it to the slave who carried it towards Alaysha.

She wished she could stop the drool collecting behind her teeth, and had to swallow repeatedly as the platter was carried close enough she could reach out and burn her fingers on the sizzling meat.

Her hand was already midair when the slave dropped to his knees, placed the plate next to him on the ground, and then lowered his palms to the moss.

Yuri was close enough for Alaysha to hear him bid another slave place the platter on the first's back.

Could she really be about to break her fast with Yuri? After all these years? Perhaps it was a ploy. Maybe they'd found number nineteen—maybe even at her site— and now Yuri would ply her with false hospitality to get to the truth and how much she knew of it.

The second servant threw the end of a hemp rope over one tree, and the other end over a second. Between the lines stretched a woven seat that, if pulled taut, could create the perfect rest for a weary warrior without him swinging in the air in an undignified way. Yuri settled into it and flicked a fringe of blond hair from his eyes. He pinned

Alaysha to her spot with them, only letting go long enough to push his fingers into the hare's belly.

He scooped stuffing into his mouth and chewed, never taking his eyes from hers. His hand found the rabbit's leg, tore it from its socket and went greasily to his mouth. Time after time, he tore the meat with his teeth, not once reaching for the tankard. Once, he paused long enough to consider a roasted egg. His lean fingers lingered over it, pressed into the seeds instead and went then into his mouth, scraping against his bottom teeth. He smacked loudly, then plucked the egg from its spot and bit into it.

Alaysha knew better than to speak. Best she wait 'til he offered her some food.

The hare was nearly gone, the stuffing spread over the plate messily, his chin shining from the honey and boar fat when she realized he planned to eat the entire thing in front of her. Even so, he had not once lifted the tankard from its spot next to the servant's foot.

He burped once and held onto his stomach as though he was obscenely full. He went even slower then, and Alaysha could see the slave's thighs trembling. There was a rustling in the undergrowth close to the cook's tent, but she didn't dare even look away from her father to see what the noise was about.

Twice her stomach complained in such an undignified manner it made Yuri grin through the mash of stuffing and eggs. He made a great show of swallowing even as he managed to make it appear as though he had no need of water or ale to wash down the meat—it was enough that he willed it move easily down his throat.

He left the last leg on the plate with an egg next to it, and wiped his palm down his mouth and off his chin.

"You did not have my consent," he said.

She knew what he was talking about. "It wasn't intentional. Truly."

"There is no such thing. There is only what I will."

She couldn't keep her eyes from the meat. "I had a fright."

"You have been trained not to fear."

"Yes."

"A witch is to feel nothing. You know this."

"I know."

"You know and yet you allow yourself to put us all at risk."

She couldn't even nod.

He made a derisive sound, one that sounded somewhere between a cough and a snort. "Your nohma made you soft. It's because of her failure that you're weak." He looked at her with an expression of disdain.

Alaysha did her best to still the squirming that wanted to take over her belly. "It's not her fault."

"Then it's yours."

"Yes."

"I let you live even knowing what you were, and you repay me with danger in my own camp? You will never outlive this shame."

She hung her head. "I know."

He sat quiet for a minute letting her feel the weight of what had happened. She saw again the weeping woman, the small babe. She had only to scan the area around her to see how the water had dried up overnight so that no one could slake their thirst. She had only to notice the tankard that still sat empty, next to the plate.

"You need to bring the rain."

"I know that, too."

"Then why do you wait? Why do you do nothing while your tribe suffers?"

"The rain comes of its own power."

"That isn't true."

She knew she'd never convince him.

"What else can I do, Father?" She held her hands out, supplicating. She was as powerless to her thirst as the rest of them. More so, even. She'd had nothing to drink and less to eat, and she was weak. A faint headache throbbed behind her eyes.

He leaned sideways, letting the weave of his seat creak as it relaxed. He noticed the slave's trembling thighs and lifted the platter from his back. "Take this to my night hound," he told him. "She has only had a raw squirrel this morning."

He pushed the slave to his belly and kicked him in the stomach until he got up and retrieved the plate.

Yuri regarded Alaysha coolly. "You don't know everything, witch. You only know pieces, and even with those small bits you would argue that you know better than me."

"Then tell me."

He regarded her with a queer expression. "Why would I tell a tool where it came from, what it is to do, where I choose to put it when I'm done?"

"Is that all I am?" She didn't believe it. He was just punishing her. He couldn't be so cold; she'd seen him with his new favourite. He did love. He did.

"You are too sharp a blade to be of any good to most men. My tribe would have me believe you're too sharp even for your maker. Are you, Alaysha? Are you too sharp for even your maker to use without danger?"

Encouraged by his use of her name, she dared: "If a man is to wield a weapon, he must know it, Father."

He muttered something unintelligible in answer and picked up the empty tankard. He shook it and peered inside thoughtfully.

"If a blade could score the sky and fill this vessel with rain, it might beg careful tempering."

He got up and passed her the tankard. "'Til then, we have much work to do. The village you ended was not the village of our search and we need to regroup. While I travel to Sarum, you and Drahl will continue the search. If he finds it, do nothing. I want to be sure it is the correct village before we take it."

His attention was taken by a crackle of twigs in the brushes nearby. "And take the vermin girl with you; I'm tired of her stealing my hounds' food. The two of you will stay well away from Drahl and his scouts at night. If you are to kill without intention, better it be something of your own."

He turned from her with a lifted brow of warning and started toward his tent.

She peered into the tankard as her father disappeared beyond his tent flap and the little ferret eased into view from behind a tree. She was chewing on the hare's leg she'd obviously stolen from the hound's dish. She offered Alaysha the half egg Yuri had left with her other hand.

Saying nothing, Alaysha popped it into her mouth and chewed thoughtfully. It was incredibly delicious for a simple roasted egg, spiced with something she'd never tasted. The smell of honey and cinnamon was strong; coming as it did from the grease Ferret's hand had left on the egg. Such were the things her father ate every day while she rooted for ferns and boiled her own scavenged eggs. Even in Sarum she'd fared no better.

She had a room, yes; she had food. The first was in the hall that should have been used for dungeons, except there'd been no need to hold captives for years—not since Yuri had been on his latest campaign and had begun to use his daughter to decimate any enemy. Down within the sanctity of dank earth, past the dozens of tunnels hewn by laboring hands, with stone on three sides and torches to light the gloom was her room. She wasn't a prisoner, exactly, but neither was she welcomed. The only time she felt anywhere near normal was on campaign, and the less she was in Sarum, the more sure of herself she grew.

So, no, she fared no better, and yet the best she could do on campaign was to eat the leavings from Yuri's plate and the left-for-dogs.

She deserved more.

"Wait for me here," she told the girl, and headed toward her father's tent.

She got only as far as Bodicca's fire before the cook herself barred the way.

The woman shook her head.

"Get out of my way," Alaysha said.

"You're too young to dispute me, even if you are trained," the woman said.

"I don't mean to try to best you," Alaysha said. "I just forgot to tell him one important detail."

The woman stared at her suspiciously. "I will have him return to you."

Ferret approached then, darting toward the fire and lifting the stick that held Bodicca's meal from the rotisserie: three wild potatoes sandwiching scraps of something that looked like meat. The cook's rage was evident even before the girl had leapt over a fallen log and had pushed her way into the trees and up the hill.

"I'll wait," Alaysha told Bodicca, trying on her best somber expression.

The woman grunted and leapt to pursuit, her long legs traversing the distance in seconds, the jangling of teeth rattling in her wake. If there was to be a time, Alaysha knew it was now.

She knew as soon as she took flight, several more guards would be upon her, so she casually lifted a cauldron from the fire and made a great show of lugging it as if it were laden with food toward Yuri's tent. A foot away, she kicked at the flap and ducked in.

He was seated on the bench to her left, his three-month-old heir lying on his lap, being rocked side to side. Alaysha expected him to show alarm at the sudden intrusion; instead, he smiled slowly.

"You take such unexpected chances with your life."

"Do I?"

He shrugged unconvincingly.

"I want to know," she said. "I have a right to know."

He sighed and passed the boy over to his mother, a frail looking blonde Yuri had rescued from her abusive father. Alaysha couldn't remember if the man's widow still lived. Right then, she didn't care.

"Tell me about those people"

"What do you need to know that would bring them back?"

She kept his eye. She had one good tool, now would be the time to use it.

"Those crones were all marked with tattaus."

Only his lower jaw moved and that so subtly Alaysha could have imagined it.

"Yes?" He said.

"Yes. Just like mine."

He nodded. "And you lied to me."

"I needed to."

"You don't trust me."

"I lied because I knew number nineteen was alive and I was afraid you'd send me to kill him."

"I would have."

"Why?"

Yuri paused a moment to wave away each and every servant. To the mother of his heir, he gave a brief kiss on the forehead and whispered in her ear. She left with the boy pressed against her bosom, and as she brushed past, Alaysha could see the drawn look to the skin of the babe's hands. Dehydrated.

She thought she would be sick.

Yuri caught her staring at the frail boy.

"She has no milk for him," he said, and he looked pained.

"Still, he must be strong," Alaysha told him—not wanting to add that if he'd escaped her power, he certainly had to be so.

"He is his father's son." Yuri turned to the table beside the bench and placed his fingertips on it, spread apart, bracing. "It's time you knew," he said.

Alaysha let go a breath she wasn't sure she had been holding. Finally.

"Those people?"

"Those people are your enemies, make no mistake." He tapped all his fingertips once, twice against the wood. "And they are the enemies of this tribe. They would take my realm and break it back into the tiny fragments I pieced together."

"Is that so bad?"

One bright brow lifted scornfully. "You are young. You wouldn't remember what it was like, and you would never know how it was before you were born."

"So tell me."

He shook his head and eased down onto the bench, put his massive hands in his lap. "No sense to. The story would take too long. No rules, no laws. No respect for life."

He glanced up at her. "It was darker than despair, those times."

"And what of those people? Is this their darkness?"

He chuckled. "Those people were your mother's people. And your mother's people were the worst of the lot. They traveled from place to place, taking what they wanted. Your mother—" he stopped, swallowed. "Your mother was a woman down the line of power, a shaman's daughter not come to her own."

It was painful to hear anything about the woman she'd never known, and thrilling too. Alaysha wanted to prod him, but was afraid he'd lose his train of thought. She waited impatiently for him to continue, drew her toe across the dirt in front of her.

She watched him lick his lips. Considering, it seemed. "Still," he said after a time. "Once I realized that to conquer them was to conquer all, I knew I had to go to war. Both to save the outlying lands from their pillaging and to join the other tribes together."

Alaysha thought of the battles she'd been on with him, the deaths she'd caused. "But they didn't come easily, did they? None of them did."

"I had to continue the campaign to remind them," he said with a deft shrug.

"Ruling by fear," she murmured.

He looked at her, surprised. "Is there a better way?"

"And the shamans?"

"Yes, the crones. They had the power to destroy you, and so me."

It was pale, as stories went. Such base motivation for killing an entire tribe, but then would she have expected anything grander from Yuri, Conqueror of Hordes? Sure, the continuation of the things he built, the ego and pride of simply having been powerful was enough to keep him on the same dogged path for all his days.

He didn't seem so big.

"And number nineteen?"

He shrugged. "The last of his line, and so all hope of the power continuing is gone."

"Except for me."

He searched her eyes for something and seeming not to find it, went on. "Except for you."

"Why not tell me before?"

"An Emir who must explain is a poor leader at best. I rule from fear, remember?"

"And if I refuse to find Number nineteen?" She knew find meant kill, and she knew neither of them would have to say it.

"Drahl will find him."

She didn't want to guess how he knew nineteen was a man. Yuri had his ways. "And what will happen to me?"

His face turned cold and he looked at her without compassion. "You know only pieces, young witch, but I know it all."

She regarded him as coolly, refusing to show emotion either. "You mean you know how to finish me."

He tapped a finger to his temple. "Make no mistake, I am not a mere father; I am Yuri—Conqueror of the Hordes—and of the crones." He grinned, but there was no humor in it. "Men fear me."

She swallowed, and tried not to let her knees shake. "Men might, Father, but Father, you taught this woman not to fear."

She spun on her heel and lifted the flap of the tent. Several of his guards stood around the perimeter, near the fire, close to the tent. Bodicca stood at the center of the guard, right where her spit waited, empty without its roasting stick. They were all expressionless, arms crossed, staring at Alaysha as she stepped into the light.

She lifted her face to the sky, thinking how good a breeze would feel against her flushed skin, and noticed with some relief, it had begun to rain.

Ferret was nearly stepping on her heels as Alaysha did her best to leave her father's camp as sedately as she could. She didn't want him or any of his guard to know how it all had affected her. Ferret, on the other hand, couldn't seem to get away fast enough and when stepping on Alaysha's heels failed to propel her faster, she took to darting in front, running ahead, then having to come all the way back.

At one point, Alaysha tried to wave her off. She really wanted to be alone. She'd always known number nineteen was supposed to die, and she'd always killed for her father without question, but now it seemed wrong. A warrior—man or woman—did as was bid in war; it was what they did. It was their duty. The Emir called them to service and the thing was done. There were no questions, no regrets. Some died in service, some lived, and some retired to teaching the craft to the young. Alaysha had trained the same as the rest, except her lessons had, of necessity, been private. Several skilled men and women went down in service to training while they tried to teach the young witch the ways of offense and defense.

She let Ferret skip ahead, dodging a loose hound returning from the hunt, and watched her halt suddenly, slink to the side, and disappear into the trees.

Several of Drahl's scouts had gathered around the fire pit, lifting their open mouths to the light rain. The fire sizzled next to them, sending puffs of smoke heavenward. Alaysha paused to watch them and to brood over the dozens of people who came from their tents with hollowed gourds to collect the water. They, like Yuri, would think she had brought the rain purposely and they still wouldn't be grateful. And their lack of gratitude was still solidly set in fear.

She'd trained as a warrior over years, and in her first months, she killed daily because she couldn't control the fear that brought the power. Each day in a tilt yard past the South wall she practiced. Two men went down the first day, then two more, the next. Yuri realized after that to tell his warriors to go easy on the six-year-old and they might live.

In the end, none of those early trainers did survive. As her prowess grew, they trained her harder, fiercer. It was only a matter of time before the trainer did something that brought her fear, and then he would just suddenly stop, fall like a limb cut from a tree, and turn to the dust. And Alaysha would pluck the eyes from the soil and hoard them in a pouch she hid in a hole in her room beneath the earth.

It was a memory she would rather not have recalled. Those days when her father was trying to help her learn control, when her power was still in its infancy and confined to a few short paces, Yuri quickly realized he couldn't keep expending his trainers or his warriors, and he soon sent in slaves. They were even fiercer than the warriors, and far less decisive. That made them more frightening.

Only later did she learn they were offered freedom for themselves and their families if they could just kill the witch.

And so they trained more desperately than any trainer or warrior ever could.

She never gained full control of the ever-growing power. She was able to project it, certainly, but not call it back, and if genuinely frightened, it sometimes came upon her unawares. But she did at least learn to become desensitized to fear of attack and death. Yuri had most definitely given her that.

Maybe too much so.

Yuri's threat of her death had no effect on her, but he did not know that. In truth, she thought she'd welcome it after all this time. She had nothing left to live for. Existence was not the same thing as living.

She reached her own campsite and began gathering her things. Better to live alone than to live as a piece of air no more useful than to be inhaled and expelled without thought.

Yuri would believe at first she was off to do his bidding, and that suited her. Later, when she didn't return, he would begin to suspect the truth, and he might send Drahl to search for her.

She would find no real pleasure in killing Drahl, and she might not enjoy killing the others who would certainly come after, but she knew by then her power would have grown enough that Yuri would need an army far larger than he could even dream of.

And how would he get it without the weapon he'd relied on all these years?

So no, she would not kill again for Yuri, but she would kill for herself if she needed to. One thing he had shown her was that she could bear taking lives—so it was time she used that complacency for herself.

She had all her possessions loaded into the two baskets that hung from Barruch's back. She would grieve the loss of her seed pouches, but there was nothing that could be done about that. She would need to find Barruch some oats or grain along the way; until then, he'd have to content himself with the bitter grass he could manage until she could find good plains lands.

His back was slick with rain, and her tunic had sopped up enough water that it felt heavy on her chest. She was mounted, reins in hand, ready to go, when she remembered the girl.

She'd said nothing the entire time and Alaysha had forgotten she was even there, so lost was she in her own thoughts and miseries. She looked to where the girl sat cross-legged on the same boulder number nineteen had stretched her sleeping skin upon earlier that morning. Alaysha couldn't see the girl's skin for the mud running down her face and onto her neck, released as it was, from the plaits. Now that the rain had washed the dirt from her hair, it had loosened into a thick curtain of soft cream.

"You can come or stay," she told the girl. "But if you come, I can't guarantee you food or shelter. I can't even guarantee you safety." She wasn't sure she wanted company, but she did know, now that someone had spent time with her, she felt less lonely.

The girl brightened at once and hopped down from the stone. "I don't have any of that now, so what's the difference?"

She ran to the horse and lifted a knee.

"What of your brother?"

The girl shrugged. "What is an absent brother to a present sister?"

Alaysha reached down, one hand under the girl's armpit, the other beneath the bent knee, and hauled her up. She settled the girl in front and gave Barruch's neck a gentle slap.

"I should call you something," Alaysha told the girl.

"I haven't used my birth name for so long, it wouldn't seem right."

"What did your captor call you?"

The girl leaned against Alaysha's chest; warmth from her back and Alaysha's stomach combined and warmed them both. Even though the rain kept up, neither shivered as Barruch plodded along. After a while, the girl answered her question without emotion and Alaysha's face burned when she heard the words.

"Commander Drahl called me Ferret," she said without emotion.

"Then I shall have to call you by a name you like."

"Let me think about it," the girl said. "It has to be the right one."

"Indeed it does," Alaysha murmured, but at the same time she was already turning over this new piece of information. No wonder the girl had disappeared each time Drahl was near. But in truth, she didn't think the man would even care if he knew his runaway was still close by. She doubted he had ever given thought to the girl and her brother. After all, they were nothing. Maybe less than nothing. Some captors were greedy for slaves, possessing them with a sense of entitlement. Some used their slaves well. Others didn't care one way or the other because to do so would be to place a value on them as a person. Drahl was that way.

Still, she hadn't the heart to hurt the girl, and so she didn't contradict her.

They rode in silence from camp, back in the direction of the village. She and the girl could easily overnight at the oasis for the days it took to dig the old women out from beneath the hut. She doubted Yuri would look for her too soon, and would only grow concerned that his best blade had gotten lost when she didn't return with reports. He would simply assume for a while he'd successfully bullied her once again into doing his bidding.

That meant she had one—maybe two—phases of the moon. She could be well away then and Sarum would be a bitter memory. She could forage as she always did for food for a while, but she hoped to come upon a space she could plant and hunt. She had a sword, but no bow. She didn't have a knife to skin any prey, but perhaps she could find a trader to swap the remaining garnet chips from her tunic.

She was beginning to feel optimistic when the girl interrupted her thoughts.

"Someone is following us."

"How do you know this when I don't?"

"Because I'm used to hiding. The person stays far enough in the trees that you wouldn't think to look, but he stops now and then when he thinks we'll see him. It's almost as though he wants you to know."

"And you know it's a him?"

"Yes."

"Is it Drahl?"

The girl shook her head. "It's the man from this morning."

Indeed. And what should she do, knowing number nineteen was so close? Acknowledge him, call him out, run away from him?

No. Best to stay the course. He'd come out when the time was right. For now, she felt it oddly comforting to have two other souls with her even if one was dodging through the trees. She felt connected in a way she hadn't enjoyed since her nohma died.

Nohma. Yuri had spoken of her as though she was a failure, but Alaysha knew it wasn't true. She'd been the only person who dared live with the witch, feeding her, teaching her. Loving her.

With Nohma's death began Alaysha's life of constant regret. After the only woman to love her succumbed to the power, Alaysha couldn't care who else it took. Until then, she'd done battle for her father half a dozen times. Nohma knew about the seeds and let her keep them. She said it was good and just to ponder over lives taken, that it should never be easy to kill. That each pair of eyes meant a dozen lives, grieving ones, seeping out enough water to flush the bodies back to rights. That Alaysha should never forget the person remaining who had lost loved ones to war.

She'd been six then, a young girl kept apart from her father's people and nursed by a woman who fed her from a garden she planted and fowl she'd raised herself. A goat supplied milk and cheese and at the end of the season, salted meat for the winter. They saw only each other except for the continual guard, the endless stream of trainers, and the people she killed when her father fetched her.

It had been the happiest Alaysha could ever remember being.

"What's got you so tense," the girl asked, sitting straighter. They were coming close enough to the village that Alaysha could see the smudge of the first body on the horizon. The vegetation had stopped like a line had been drawn, and the soil was wet from the rains. She noted the position of the sun. They had been traveling for hours, plodding along, and she was getting hungry.

"I was just thinking," Alaysha said.

"Nothing bad, I hope."

"There is no bad. There just is."

"Will he come out now?"

Alaysha did her best not to turn in the saddle to where she suspected number nineteen lurked. He had followed—Barruch's pace had been easy enough, but he'd not made any attempt to truly hide. She gauged him capable of being invisible when he wanted; and so he must have wanted her to know he was there.

Now she was close to the last stand as she'd begun to think of it, she wasn't sure she was ready to share it with her passenger. Not sure the girl would understand. Alaysha looked to the left and saw the wavering relief of the oasis.

"Looks like the perfect place for us to lie down for the night, what do you think?"

"It would have to be better than what's ahead."

So she had seen the desolation they were moving into. Smart girl. Alaysha kneed Barruch sideways and within moments, excited by the smell of fresh grass and water, he picked up his pace. It wasn't long before they were off his back and picking their way beneath tree limbs and between brambles that turned out to be blackberry bushes.

Alaysha reached into her basket and pulled out her wooden bowl. "Collect what you can," she told the girl. "I'm going to see about a fire and a good spot to set up."

The girl nodded at a tree over Alaysha's shoulder. "Peaches."

How had she missed that before? Already Alaysha's mouth was watering. She noticed more too, that she hadn't on her first visit: wild onions, hazelnut bushes, even a fair sized beehive with liquid gold oozing from the hole in a large beech tree.

"How lucky are we?"

The girl's mouth was filled with berries, her lips purple.

"Never mind answering." Alaysha couldn't help chuckling. They'd have roasted nut mash and onions for supper and honeyed fruit as a treat. Now. All they needed was water.

"Collect some nuts too," she told the girl. "And pull those onions." She pointed to a spiked patch of green, thready leaves. She plucked four peaches from the tree and tossed them to the girl. "Think you can collect some honey without getting stung?"

"Of course."

"Good. We'll eat wonderfully this eve."

The girl thumbed over her shoulder. "What about him?"

Number nineteen stood next to Barruch, his palm against the horse's flank. He wore his black hair tied back, slicked with mud.

Alaysha shook her head. "What is it with you people and dirt?"

He and the girl both shrugged in unison, but it was nineteen who spoke. "Keeps the hair out of my eyes."

Alaysha looked to her girl for confirmation, and the girl nodded. "Me, too. Don't have to worry about not seeing what you need to."

It made a sort of grudging sense, but something within made Alaysha shudder at the thought.

"Do you know where the water is?"

Nineteen grinned. "Of course."

Alaysha waited, but he said no more.

"Well, are you going to show me?"

He stepped into the clearing and bent to the bowl the girl had set on the ground, filled to the brim with berries. He popped two at a time into his mouth, and grimaced. "Got a sour one," he said.

"I'm glad to hear it. Now. The water?"

"Just behind you, through the bushes."

She grunted and stalked off, parting a few thorn bushes, and startling a garter snake that slithered across her instep. She heard a chuckle from behind. "Careful," he said. "There're snakes."

She guessed he'd done the same when he was here. Rocks were plentiful on the faint path, perfect for nests and warmth. She wasn't scared of serpents, but neither was she overeager to step on one. She paid careful attention as she padded forward, once seeing a writhing mass that must have begun as a clutch of eggs. Well, if snakes chose to nest here, there must be plenty of game. Maybe she'd rouse a quail or two from some hatchlings and be able to roast a few tender chicks. Better yet, an entire family over a spit with some of that honey. More perfect still, two fat, large breasted partridge with meat to fill her belly for days. Her stomach again reminded her it had been at least a day since she'd had anything decent to eat.

She heard the sure sound of rushing water and pushed aside the last of the bracken. To her amazement, what showed itself was a narrow waterfall emptying into a large pool. Blue moss grew on the stones around the edge, and layered on the marsh edges were cattails; large and thick as her arm. Three ducks gurgled to each other in a shallow feeder pool just to the side. A large bullfrog jumped off the rock next to her and plopped into the water to swim and disappear in seconds within the grasses.

The nut mash and onion meal just upgraded to frog legs and roast duck. But first, water.

She lowered her face into the pool and slurped without using her hands. It was sweet and fresh and cold, enough to make her back teeth ache, and still she kept drinking 'til her belly was bloated.

No wonder nineteen had come here when his village was under attack. He had everything he needed to survive.

She scouted the edge of the pool for stray frogs and with each one she found, thwacked it solidly against the stone, then onto a pile while she could forage for the cattail roots. They'd be bitter if boiled alone, but if she could cut them up and mix them with peach slices, the fruit juice might cut the starch enough to make them palatable. She had seven dug and four frogs waiting when she realized number nineteen was foraging on the other side of the pond.

She watched him quietly for a few moments; he was focused as a scavenger, peering just beyond his feet for several seconds before stooping and rising with something in his hands. Then, absorbed in his task, and seeming to choose the spot with specific care, he placed his booty on the ground. She realized she enjoyed watching him, the lithe way his muscles moved as he bent and raised and reached. He had a powerful looking torso, one that held heat like the embers of a fire, if she remembered well. That night beneath her fur, she'd slept sounder than she could remember in ages, and she knew it was because he slept next to her, his legs thrown over hers at night, his palm possessive against her stomach. She touched her belly where his palm had been, and felt a flush fill her cheeks.

She gathered her own treasures and headed over to where he once again bent and straightened. When he caught sight of her, he smiled widely.

"We're in luck," he said.

"We are." She showed him her armload. He looked at it with something akin to tolerance. Not the delight she'd expected. She felt oddly deflated.

"You don't like roast frog legs?"

He shrugged. "In a pinch, maybe."

"And you've done better?"

He grinned again. "Best, not better." He indicated a hollowed gourd filled with writhing fat yellow worms.

The water filling her mouth had nothing to do with hunger. "You're greening me."

He shook his head. "They taste like roast boar and fowl both at the same time."

"You eat them?" She thought if he offered her a wriggling pit of pus, she'd have to end him. "Raw?"

"You can have yours raw, I like mine roasted. Get some of those cattail leaves." He pointed to the crop of tall leaves to her right at the marshy edge.

She trudged over and started pulling on them.

"No, no; not like that." He made a sweeping motion. "Cut them."

Cut them. Well, easy enough if you had a blade to hand, which she didn't. Rather than prolong the discussion, she simply tried to tear them across at the widest end. He clucked at her disapprovingly and came close enough to put his hand on hers. "Like this," he said, and guided her hand to twist as she peeled, and soon, she had the knack. He didn't move away from her, though, even when she got good at it. She could feel him close, hear his breathing. She wanted to turn and step into him. What she did was brandish a bunch of limp fronds at him.

"Good girl," he said, beaming. He touched her fingers when he reached for them and then she was in his arms. She hadn't meant to, just sort of stepped and there he was, his hands full of leaves, holding on to her back, pressing her even closer. He smelled of earth and old smoke. His mouth tasted of berries and she found herself wondering what he would taste like after honeyed peaches.

He broke away with reluctance. "Too bad you have but the one skin to keep us warm. Maybe we can find a way to share it."

She knew she'd like nothing better. "I'm not sure three would fit." She laughed and made to throw the leaves she still had in her hand onto the pile. "Oh no," she said. "Your worms are trying to wriggle away."

He spit out a few words she didn't understand and then was bobbing about, hunched over, weaving this way and that as he tried to catch them.

In the end, they both worked their way back to the clearing to set about preparing the meal. When Ferret saw the grubs, she exclaimed with such glee, Alaysha thought it must have been a silent conspiracy to trick her all along.

"You don't eat those," she said to the girl.

The girl shrugged much as Number Nineteen had. "Of course not."

"Then what's all the excitement for?"

"You've never heard of the magics of the Meroshi?"

Alaysha watched the youth standing beside her. He seemed pretty ignorant too.

"What is it?"

The girl reached for the bowl and set it down next to a prepared fire pit. "Meroshi was our people's shaman before I was born. He was said to be able to see at night and become invisible."

Alaysha set the cattail fronds next to the bowl and noticed a pile of berries and nuts as well. "And? I can see at night. What's so special?"

"He would know his enemies in the dark and it was all because of this worm."

Alaysha looked down at the wriggling mess. "It has special powers?"

The girl nodded.

"It's said to be the only thing that could overtake Meroshi during his most vulnerable hour."

Number Nineteen was growing interested finally. He'd already shifted foot to foot, and now was squatting next to the pile of yellow grubs, his fingers in the middle of the mess, flicking them apart, inspecting them one at a time.

"We've eaten them in my tribe for decades."

The girl shot him a look of disbelief. "And you've not yet learned of their powers?"

He lifted one shoulder offhandedly. "They taste amazing roasted over a smoky flame. I'd say that's a pretty good power."

The girl gave him a wary glance. "You eat them?"

He nodded.

"Well. No wonder you've not witnessed its magics. Meroshi came from a long line of powerful shamans. He could call flame from the sky, make winds howl, and the earth shake."

"Oh." He snorted. "My tribe can do the same."

Alaysha stole a look at him. Was he lying? The girl slapped his hand away from the worms and he chuckled. "So what was this Meroshi's best power if I have shamans who can do the same?"

"Do your shamans have the power to become invisible?"

He scoffed. "In the dark, we are all invisible."

The girl shrugged and sat down next to the fire pit, adding dead leaves to the top. She went silent and absorbed in preparing for a rousing blaze. The tension grew unbearable. Alaysha could tell the girl wanted to be pressed for the remainder of the story, and as equally, Nineteen didn't want to ask. She let them alone, trying to quell her own curiosity by digging for her tinder bundle and setting the fire, but after a few long moments, the curiosity got the best of her.

"Tell us more."

The girl reached for a grub and pinched it between her fingers. The skin of it broke and let loose an oozing mass of white innards. Not yellow as expected, or even green. Just plain white worm meat.

"It was known by our people that the only way to defeat Meroshi was to come at him just before dawn, when it was the darkest and when he was at his most vulnerable."

The girl scraped the carcass on the grass. "This grub would allow the assassin extra sight, far better than any warrior's vision." She looked pointedly at Nineteen. "Mash these down—five or six of them—and paint three stripes of their fluid beneath each eye and you are granted special sight."

"That's ridiculous."

The girl grinned. "Go right ahead and eat them, but save us some just in case we need them." She reached for Alaysha's tinder bundle and added moss to it, blowing on it to get the smoke moving. She spoke to Alaysha. "Would you help me gather the honey? I need a boost into the tree."

Alaysha nodded and uncurled her legs. She stood and reached for the girl's hand. "I can't imagine those peaches and berries without a honey drizzle now I've decided to have it."

The tree wasn't terribly high, but the way the girl made several attempts to climb with no avail set suspicion into Alaysha's spine. She wove her fingers together and bid the girl step into the cup they made. They were well away from hearing, but Alaysha whispered anyway.

"Could your shamans bring rain too?" She had to know. Were these powers more common than she thought; were there others like her?

The girl giggled as she placed her foot into Alaysha's hands. "Meroshi was lucky if he could put food into his own mouth."

"But—"

The girl's eyes caught Alaysha's conspiratorially. "He was a madman in my village. We had no shaman. Only warriors. Cunning warriors." She peered over Alaysha's shoulders. "Don't look, but another Meroshi trap has just been set." She sprang up and clambered into the tree then waved the tinder moss over the hole. Smoke curled in and around and a few bees seeped drowsily from the entrance.

"What will happen then?" Alaysha asked.

The girl cupped her palm and reached slowly into the crevice. "You'll see come nightfall."

"Tell me about your warriors."

"They're fierce. They fear nothing. Care for nothing. They move in the dark and in the light with equal prowess."

The pride in her voice was almost painful to hear, knowing that she was right now running from her captor. Alaysha thought back to battle sixteen. It hadn't seemed particularly fierce. In fact, except that she had to send the power out over and over again to meet the waves of new fighters, it had seemed very easy.

"Then how did Yuri capture such grand warriors?"

The girl looked at her, no emotion in her face. "He didn't capture them. You killed them."

Alaysha found she couldn't keep the girl's gaze. She thought back to that battle and the warriors she'd murdered at her father's behest. She wondered just how much this girl knew of her power—how much she'd seen or heard. It would explain her complacency back at Yuri's camp, when she'd seen the result of the power on that poor babe, when the power had drained the ready water from the pots and skins. And if this girl had some inkling of the power, then how many others?

Chapter 8

It was a long wait 'til nightfall, but an enjoyable one. Number Nineteen had somehow gotten the fire to a perfect blaze to roast the frog legs and cattail-wrapped worms. With peaches and berries bubbling happily in a syrupy bowl of honey at the edge of the fire, and sliced cattail roots frying on flat rocks, all they had to do was stretch before the flames and relax.

The feast was as grand as anything she'd eaten, and she wasn't sure if it was the food or the chatter and laughter of the other two that put a perpetual smile on her face. It could have been the way her leg touched Number Nineteen every now and then, and the way he made small, but frequent attempts to touch her. All she knew was she was happy, and she'd not felt happy since her nohma died.

No one mentioned or even glanced at the gourd outside the edge of the fire, purposefully hidden between small stones and branches, but Alaysha knew it was filled with a soup of wriggling yellow bodies.

"So, what of your tribe," she asked him. He had licked the last of his fingers clean of honey and lay stretched sideways to the fire, his black hair loose and hanging in his eyes. From where Alaysha sat, those eyes looked like lit honey. She reached out to wipe a bit of peach from his chin.

"Your tribe, you mean," he said.

She shrugged. "So you say."

He rubbed his stomach. "Our tribe is made of four major clans. I am Fire Clan. You are Water. Didn't your nohma tell you this?" He sounded as though he couldn't believe she'd not been taught such a simple thing. She felt stung at the tone, much as she would if a bee had bit her.

When he noticed she wasn't answering, he rolled onto his back.

"You think you have secrets from me," he said to the growing dark.

"It's all I have," she murmured. She and the girl were huddled close together, bracing against the chill at their backs.

"You have less than you think, then. Don't you want to know where you came from?"

"I know enough," she lied.

His low chuckle rumbled with the fire. "Your enough makes you hunger for more, but you're afraid to ask."

"I was trained not to fear."

"Then what was that you felt the night I came to you?"

She couldn't answer. It hadn't been the first time she'd accidentally let loose her power, but it had been the first time in many years. It unnerved her to think her power was getting the better of her, that she couldn't control it.

"I'll tell you what it is, Alaysha," he said. "It's the power growing in you; it's coming to its peak as you mature and it will soon overwhelm you." He craned his neck to look at her across the flame, and as the light danced on his features, she thought she saw fire within him. "You need me," he said.

She looked away, out into the shadows of the trees, and listened for Barruch's breathing in the dark to ground her, to remind her who she was and why she was here. The conversation had gone far too deep into the pits of those things she'd always longed for and been afraid of. He'd touched too far into the hollow spaces she'd spent years trying to fill with her collections.

"I always thought I needed no one," she said. It was true, wasn't it? She'd spent so many years alone, despite the companionship of this fire, she had survived without affection for so long, she knew she could manage without it again if she had to.

As if realizing he'd gone too far, he pointed to the first star winking in the sky, the one high above them, already brighter than the pale moon. "I was named after that light."

Alaysha's attention piqued. She knew what her nohma called that first light of the evening—that brightest purplish light that lasted far into the early morning. It was the Eye of Yenic, she'd said, peering to watch over his beloved Yen, the soft belly of the earth below him, until the sun could care for her properly.

"And here I was calling you nineteen," she said, forcing a laugh.

"Nineteen?"

She hung her head and felt a curtain of hair mercifully cover her face. "Yes. The one that got away."

He thought for a moment. "Nineteen," he said after a time. "After the eighteen you killed."

"Yes," was all she could say.

He shifted to sit cross-legged. "You counted wrong," he murmured. "There were twenty."

She squirmed when she thought about it. "Yes. One woman was pregnant."

"My sister," he said.

Alaysha fell silent, the sense of shame covering her like a fur. It had been war, so she thought. She'd not known the village was filled with citizens. Not until she'd sent the power out, thirsting for whatever water it could find. She'd let it go and traveled the paths with the energy—down to the ground, along the grasses, up bare feet and legs, through tear ducts. When the power got to the unborn, it was already too late.

Its eyes would have been amber, she realized. Were amber.

"I remember her," she whispered.

"My sister?"

"No. Your niece."

Yenic said nothing at that, but he rose from his spot at the fire and kicked the place where the worms rested in their gourd. He reached down with his elegant, but callused fingers and lifted the bowl from its spot and trudged into the underbrush. He disappeared in the cascade of leaves and branches.

The girl beside her shifted. "I feel bad for what's about to happen to him now," she said.

"I feel nothing," Alaysha responded, seeing his reaction. She hadn't wanted to hurt him and now she had, she wanted to take it back. She wanted to return to the sense that those things didn't matter. She couldn't afford to feel anything. It wasn't a warrior's place to question or feel guilt about killing on command. If one did, then a whole life would be spent recovering from a single deed.

"Is he telling the truth about his tribe and yours being the same?"

Alaysha nodded. "I think so. My father told me much the same."

"Is that why we're here?"

Alaysha sighed. She wasn't sure anymore. She'd wanted to know the connection at first, but now she thought all she really wanted was to get away. What did it matter that she belonged to a nearly extinct tribe.

"We're here because we needed a place to rest," she said and pulled the girl closer.

"Did you really kill his people?"

"I did."

"How could you?"

"How could I not?" Alaysha shrugged. "I was not my own. Much as you aren't."

"I ran away, and I am my own now."

Alaysha squeezed her tightly, enjoying the feeling that for once she had the comfort of another body next to hers. Scrawny though it might be, it was a great consolation.

"As I am my own, now, too."

"Maybe I should go stop him."

Alaysha held the girl back when she started to pull away.

"I doubt he wants anyone around at the moment. Whatever it is you've done to him with those worms, it'll keep for a while."

Yenic was gone a long time; Alaysha was startled to find she had fallen asleep and was cushioning the girl's head as she also slept. At times, though she'd felt herself nodding off next to the heat, she hadn't thought she'd actually succumbed to the night. She hadn't remembered feeding the fire either and yet it roared merrily on.

She heard him coming long before she saw him, and Barruch whickered noisily when the bushes rustled.

At first, she wasn't sure what she was seeing, but it looked like fireflies hovering in six straight lines behind the lacy cover of leaves. They lifted and moved together left and right, bobbing up and down, all in unison. Then they shot towards the ground and the stomping racket of feet in too much a hurry to care about making noise rattled across the air.

"Something's wrong," Yenic was saying, his voice a hoarse, pained noise. "What have you done to me?"

Alarmed now, Alaysha pushed the girl's head from her lap and jumped to her feet, taking the strides she needed to grab her sword from her bundle. Yenic broke through the tree cover, the six stripes on his cheeks more obvious now, not fireflies as she'd thought, but the phosphorescent yellow color of the grub's skin. His hands were aloft as he looked at them, the yellow shining brightly in the dark on the tips of his fingers and smeared on his palm.

A low chuckle came from behind her, stopping Alaysha in her tracks. She turned to the girl to see her moving towards Yenic with her hand over her mouth, trying to keep the laughter in.

"Can you still see, Yenic? Can you see in the dark?"

"No better than I did before." He didn't sound impressed.

"Does it burn yet?"

"You mean it's going to burn?"

"And steal your vision once your eyes swell shut."

Yenic made a noise between a groan and a scream, then stumbled about, feeling his way around as though he was already blind. "Shouldn't you at least help me?"

"I can take you to the water. That should prevent the burning."

"And the swelling?"

"Oh, yes. Of course, the swelling." The girl snickered and Alaysha sent her a reproachful look that sent the black eyes downcast so quick it was obvious she realized she'd played a poor game.

"You did this to him; you should help."

"I didn't do anything," came the protest, but the girl minced toward him and reached out for his hand when she was close enough. "Here, I'll help rinse it all off. But we'd better hurry before you start seeing things."

His shouts rose an octave and mixed with words Alaysha had never heard even in her rides with the most swarthy of warriors. The only intelligible thing she could make out were his last, frantic ones.

"Seeing things?"

The dry response was nearly lost in the bushes as the girl answered. "Where do you think Meroshi's power came from? Magic?"

"I believed you," Yenic's tone turned pouting.

"Of course you did. It's a story we tell every outsider, knowing they'll try it. So we can see them coming should they decide to attack, and if they do attack, they fight the shadows of their night terrors rather than any one of us." She guided him away from the fire toward the waterfall and Alaysha could hear Yenic's plaintive protest that he wasn't an outsider.

The girl's matter-of-fact reply came right on its heels. "Maybe not, but how often do you think I get a chance to tell that story? Why even the youngest of us knows better than to play with the dreamer's worm."

Alaysha watched them go and settled back down near the fire. If the girl knew such a use for a grub that Yenic's kind did nothing but eat, then her tribe must know things most didn't. Alaysha had never seen the repugnant thing before, let alone know to eat it.

It was one more thing that reminded her of how ignorant she was. All she'd ever known was battle and loneliness, duty and despair.

She resolved again to find out as much as she could—and to get as far away from her father as she could. Now she'd tasted freedom without the burden of duty, she rather enjoyed it.

As it turned out, Yenic's eyes were sore enough that he lay curled next to the fire when they returned. The girl tried her best to coax conversation with him, but he only grunted at her and rubbed at his eyes.

"Don't worry," she said. "It'll only hurt for a little while. We got it all off in plenty of time."

He said nothing.

"And even if we hadn't, the effects are only temporary. A day or so of hallucinations and swelling, and it's all gone again."

He blinked. "But you got it all off in time," he said blandly.

She smiled brightly. "Right."

"Right," he said and curled farther into an indignant ball and went to sleep without a further word.

She'd made a cozy spot next to the fire with her thatched mat and fur and let the girl crawl into the crook she made with the curve of her body. She heard a small sigh and thought it might have been her own. She might have shared her blanket with Yenic had things gone differently.

"He's angry," Alaysha whispered so not to disturb him.

"Yes, he's angry, but not half so angry as he'll be tomorrow night."

"Why, what happens tomorrow?" Alaysha was almost afraid to ask.

"The sun will gather on his cheeks where the stripes are and store there 'til nighttime."

"And…?"

"And he will glow as brightly tomorrow night as he does tonight."

Alaysha moaned softly. "For how long?"

"It wears off after a couple of days. The longer it stays painted on, the longer it lasts. He should stop glowing in a couple of nights."

"Does he know this?"

The girl shook her head.

Come morning, Alaysha woke to a smoky, dampened fire. She shivered beneath her fur and realized the girl was gone. She lifted her head to peer across the smoke and saw Yenic sitting on a rock, knees up, feet that were filthy from rummaging planted solidly against the stone. He was munching on a handful of what she presumed were nuts, popping one after the other into his mouth and chewing thoroughly.

He was staring straight at her and her heart made an almost audible thunk in her chest.

"Where is the girl?" she asked him.

He shrugged.

"How long have you been awake?"

"Long enough."

"What does that mean?" She wasn't sure anymore what to make of him. Was he still angry at her for killing his sister, for mentioning the unborn child?

He let one foot slide off the rock, and then the other until he stood and stretched. His rib cage lifted and Alaysha could see the way the ribbon of tattaus actually went up underneath his armpit and onto the fleshy, tender spot of his tricep.

"Do all our tribe have these tattaus?"

He shook his head and some of his hair stuck to his cheek and left strands of black beneath the faint glow of green. "Did you see tattaus on all the people you killed back there?" He jerked his head in the direction of the arid piece of land.

She thought about it. The first man had the markings, yes. And a few of the others. The crones did: theirs were identical in placement as her own. The children were clean, though. And most of the women.

"Your sister was marked."

He nodded warily, but it looked like he was trying to keep the wariness from his eyes. They still looked like benign, sweet honey.

"But hers were just open symbols." Alaysha had to think back, let her memory recall the flesh path the power had taken when it had crept over the village. She'd overlooked the detail before because it was insignificant at the time.

"Across her chin," he said.

Alaysha's fingers went involuntarily to her face, wanting to touch the narrow ribbon of ink snaking from earlobe to earlobe and across her chin. She remembered her nohma putting the marks there. It had hurt, but since Nohma had the odd tattaus too, she'd wanted them and put up with the pain. She wanted hers to be exactly the same, but Nohma wouldn't have it.

"Nohma wouldn't put mine on my back where hers were. She told me mine must be on my face."

Yenic stepped closer, as though he were testing the temperature of the water. As he came around the fire pit he lifted his arm and with the fingers of his other hand traced the tattau's path from tricep to hip. When he got close enough that Alaysha could touch him, he took her hand and placed it in the middle of his markings—near the first rib. She felt his skin pimple and laid her palm flat against it.

"I got the first mark when I was four," he told her.

"I was young too," she said.

"The Arms of the Witch are tattaued like this because we are her reach. Her protection. Our arms are in service to her." He met her eyes and held them with his own so intensely, she could barely swallow.

"How many?"

"One for each witch."

"And my Nohma?"

"She shoulders the burden of caring for the witch."

Alaysha nodded. The symbolism made sense. She let her hands search the markings while he stood, silently letting her trace one to the next. They were quite beautiful up close, the way the skin showed through against the black band surrounding them. It must have taken hours to craft such a long line with such intricate detail and symbols. Her fingers reached the base of his armpit and she felt him shudder.

"I'm sorry. That spot tickles, doesn't it?"

His voice sounded as though it came from a dark pit when he answered. "No. Not ticklish at all." He let his arm fall and reached to touch the corner of her mouth, then his fingers trailed the length of her tattau, stopping at her ear. He cupped the back of her head and she thought for a second that the clump of air that had somehow lodged in her chest would keep her from speaking.

"Why are mine on my chin?"

He smiled and leaned forward. The feel of his lips against her forehead made her chest tight.

"Because yours is the burden of swallowing our sins." His hand left her nape and traveled down her back. She felt herself begin to mold against him almost as though she were made of oil and was finding the curves of his body like she was meant to. When his palm pulled her hips closer to his, she let herself step into the embrace and enjoy the warmth of his body against hers.

"It's a difficult burden, Alaysha," he said into her hair. "But you don't have to suffer it alone."

She felt the tension leave at his words and hadn't realized her muscles had been coiled and ready to run. If they'd ever felt relaxed, she was sure it had been during childhood, before her first battle, and it felt good to let them ease into each other, one fiber connecting to the next without worry that they'd need to fight or run. Without thinking, she put her arms around his waist and rested her cheek against his bare chest. She could hear his heart beating within like a happy fire sending flames roaring over thick logs.

"I've been alone for so long," she said. "Ever since Nohma…" She didn't want to say it. She couldn't.

He pulled away just enough that he could peer down at her and searched her eyes with his own. "What about your nohma?"

"I killed her."

He looked truly perplexed. "But you couldn't."

She stepped back and leaned to pick up a stick to poke the fire. She'd admitted it, finally, but she didn't think she could take the admonishment. She hadn't meant to, after all. She stirred the ashes and lifted a charred blocks to allow it air so the fire could catch beneath it.

"Alaysha?"

She would answer, but she wouldn't look at him. "I did. I killed her."

"You couldn't." He grasped her by the shoulder and twisted her away from the fire. "Her tattaus, her blood, would have protected her."

Now it was her turn to be confused. "Her blood?"

"Yes. Alaysha. Didn't you know she was your mother's sister? She was your blood witch."

Alaysha ran her memory back as many paths as she could as she stood there. It didn't make sense. She'd killed her, she knew it. She remembered it.

"I don't understand," she said.

"You are young," he said and took the stick from her. In his hands the fire leapt to ready flame.

"How do you do that so easily?"

He grinned at her. "I can't tell you all my secrets."

"It seems you are keeping a good many." She held her hands out to the flame.

"I have a few, yes," he agreed.

There were so many questions already roiling around in her head, she barely knew what to ask. How would she ever find a way to sort them all out? Yet something was bothering her more than anything else. Something he'd said kept trying to creep back into her consciousness.

"Your sister had tattaus across her chin."

He nodded but he wouldn't look into her eyes. "She was being tattaued. We thought she had plenty of time to get them finished."

"I got to her before she could have the black filled in?"

"Yes."

"You said the symbols and their placement were relevant."

Again he nodded.

"So your sister was a witch."

He sighed as though he'd been holding his breath. "Yes. She would have been. But not nearly as powerful as you."

He looked at her so strangely she thought she must have said something wrong. He reached for her and she went to him without thinking and stepped into his embrace.

"You have more power than you can know. I don't blame you, Alaysha."

She thought she heard herself sob but knew it couldn't be true; she'd never once cried over all the lives she had taken. Not once. A warrior did not feel. A warrior did not allow emotion to keep her from her task.

She felt the warmth of his breath on her cheek before she felt his touch. He kissed her just at the rise of each cheek, where she knew tears had pooled, and then he brushed her eyes with his lips, capturing the fluid as it leaked out.

"You're so beautiful," he murmured.

His mouth claimed hers tentatively at first, then took it with such confidence, as if he owned her lips and already knew the way they curved, how they would move against his, when her mouth would gasp in release. She responded so similarly, she felt herself losing the will to stand and even as she thought she would let go, she felt his arms beneath her knees and around her waist and she was laid down, against the fur. His hand roamed her hips and legs, stroked her back. She couldn't stop herself from pressing against him and feeling every inch of his body against hers, and yet it still wasn't close enough.

Barruch made a sound somewhere between a whinny and a snort, and it was enough to remind Alaysha that they were not truly alone; the girl could have returned. She pulled away and scrabbled to her feet, breathless and feeling as though she'd narrowly escaped some danger. Yenic lay on his back with a short grin playing at the corners of his mouth. He put his hands behind his head and for a second, she wanted to strike him for his arrogance but remembered how badly she wanted to feel his mouth on hers again, and ended up scurrying away to hide the blush she knew had taken her cheeks.

Barruch stomped his front feet impatiently, thankfully giving her time to recover and digest all she now knew.

She moved to put her palm on his nose where a small spot of white showed, and he lowered it to avoid her touch. She went to pat his chest and he huffed away.

"Come now, old man, you can't say you're unhappy with me."

He merely blinked and swatted at her with his tail.

Spending time and attention on her horse gave Alaysha a few minutes to gather her thoughts. She'd never once questioned Nohma about her past. True, it was odd, now she thought it, that her nurse treated her so familiarly. But she'd never once indicated they were related. And if it was true that she was protected by blood from Alaysha's young powers, then how was Alaysha able to take her life?

She ran her hand down Barruch's neck, letting her memory take her places she had never forgotten, but had chosen to bury. That night when she was just six, her name day, actually, she'd been allowed to feed her new colt and was so excited she couldn't stop talking. She'd wanted to run to her father and thank him, but Nohma held her back. He wouldn't be interested in gratitude, Nohma told her. He was only interested in getting his own mount back—and safely out of killing distance. She'd already destroyed several of his horses.

That too, was true. Forced to ride in a basket slung off the side of his mount for years, she'd killed plenty, not the least the horse upon which she was saddled when she unleashed her thirst.

"He was tired of walking back to camp with you on his back," Nohma told her. And so in the last battles, she'd been pitched forward with Nohma in the saddle, armed scouts to the left and right, a full armament in the back.

Only Nohma, Alaysha, and the poor sacrificial beast riding forward to greet the opposition.

In those days, her power was unpredictable, yes, and far from the mature ability to kill at long distances. She was deprived of food and water for days before battle and sent, afraid, into the perimeter to let loose her primal fear of thirsting to death.

And men fell.

And the horse beneath her fell.

And usually Nohma was left standing to carry her back to the camp while the warriors went in to gather the slaves. But that last time, that last battle when they'd learned to leave the horse far behind the battle lines, with Nohma standing beside her, confident in the history that proved she was the only one capable of living in proximity with the witch, that last battle Nohma fell. And no matter how long Alaysha stood in the rain in the aftermath, the seeds of her eyes never took root and grew back into the woman who loved her.

So the blood hadn't protected her. And the symbols were not strong enough.

She turned to Yenic, wanting to tell him he was wrong, but standing next to him was the girl; she'd come back from her foraging, obviously.

But she was not alone.

Chapter 9

"This is my brother," the girl said. She looked up to the swarthy man at her side. He was tall, much taller than Yenic and several inches thicker. His hair was matted in mud so that it was all back off his face and temples. His eyes were as green as a wolf pup's and looked to be about as predictable. His arm wasn't slung over the girl's shoulder so much as it was clenching her bicep in a meaty hand.

Yenic looked as though he was about to hurl himself across the few feet and use his own shoulder as a battering ram to the solid wall of stomach that was the brother, and looking at the way the interloper was holding onto the girl, Alaysha couldn't say she blamed him.

"Welcome," she said, not sure what else she should say; after all, the man was this girl's kin.

Rather than act pleased over the hospitality, he sneered at her and pushed the girl forward.

"Tell her," he said.

Alaysha noticed the skinny legs trembling, the furtive way the girl kept looking into the trees. She suspected there was more to the visitor's party than what the youth was letting on.

"Edulph wants to know what you are."

Alaysha had to tear her gaze from the girl's trembling shoulders. "If you've hurt her…"

The boy spat. "Aedus doesn't need pain to be reminded where she comes from."

"Aedus?" So that was the girl's name. Alaysha caught and held the girl's eye. Yes. It was true.

"Where'd you come from?" she asked Aedus.

The girl started to speak, but got shoved from behind. She stumbled forward and had to catch herself from falling. Edulph spoke for her instead.

"Doesn't matter. What does matter is how you're going to help us kill your father."

It would be laughable if he didn't seem so earnest. Alaysha sensed Yenic taking subtle steps toward her and Barruch's breathing had shifted. It was shallower, ready to bolt if need be.

"You want to kill Yuri." Even speaking it didn't make it sound more sensible.

"I want to kill Yuri and enslave his people like he did mine."

"You'll never manage it. Yuri's people would never serve." She didn't think she'd have to add how difficult it would be to assassinate the conqueror of the hordes. He'd not got that way through being a docile man, and did not manage to lead for so long by being accessible. Alaysha thought of Bodicca and the men whose teeth circled her forearms.

She decided to wait out this strangely ambitious brother, reason with him somehow. She didn't care, in the end whether he made war on Yuri or whether he went his own way and forgot about his vengeance. It was no concern of hers. But for the girl. She couldn't stand the way this brother acted as though Aedus was a possession to be used. She glared at him. "I don't care what you do, but you will leave your sister to decide if she wants a part in it or not."

Edulph grabbed Aedus's scrawny arm and twisted her backwards, so she was pinioned next to him.

"Let her go." Heat flooded Alaysha's neck, the anger boiling in her chest and needing out. She took an angry stepped forward, intending to thrash the daylights from this insipid bastard once and for all. She would have stormed the fire's perimeter when she felt Yenic's hand on her shoulder. She gave him a questioning look.

He ignored it and addressed Edulph. "What is it you really want? We have no quarrel with you."

Edulph snorted. "You have a quarrel with Yuri, though."

Yenic nodded. "Maybe, but why do we care that you do? Go your way. Make your war. We have no stake in it."

Edulph inclined his head at Alaysha. "I've seen her. I've seen what she can do. Out there." He jerked his head towards the arid land that was once Yenic's village. "I've been with the scouts, with the warriors over the years. I've seen the desolation she's left behind. Not a single arrow shot. Not a torch put to grass."

Alaysha's stomach began to squirm. She'd been careful never to have anyone witness the things she'd done, but they had certainly witnessed the aftermath. It would be easy for someone to think, to believe, that the massacres were easy.

"You have no idea," she said.

"I have some idea. Enough idea to know you have magic. Aedus has said the same."

It was Yenic's turn to interrupt. "She told us there is no such thing as magic." He shot Aedus a scolding eye. "So why would you believe any exists?"

Alaysha had had enough of the diplomacy. She didn't care what the hooligans believed. "Just let the girl decide and be gone." She stomped over to Barruch to get her sword. A dozen men stepped from the shadows.

"Careful, fools," she said. "I'm trained."

She heard a laugh come from Edulph and she whirled to face him. "It would not do to provoke me."

"Or what? You and your boy will fight my fifty men? Please do. Please show me."

Aedus spoke in a shaking voice. "Please, Edulph. You have no idea."

"Oh, I do have some idea, Aedus. And more since your little stories."

"How much did you tell, Aedus?" Alaysha asked. She traveled the days of memory to see how often and how much the girl might know of her power.

The girl shrugged helplessly, and Alaysha guessed that, excited to see the brother she'd been pining for, she told him everything she knew, never guessing or caring what Edulph's plans would be. And just what were those plans?

"What is it you want, then?" She demanded.

"You."

Yenic was there in a flash, holding his arm against her chest, and for a moment, Alaysha barely cared that his fingers were digging into her shoulder.

"You think I'll kill my entire tribe for you?" She wouldn't think about the irony of it. She just wouldn't.

Edulph grinned. "I don't think. I know." He tapped his temple and made a grab for Aedus's hand. Before Alaysha or Yenic could do anything, he had shoved the whole of her palm deep into the flames.

Alaysha wasn't sure if the piercing scream came from Aedus or not, but she was painfully aware that her own mouth was open wide and that her chest hurt. Her ears hurt. Her throat hurt. And just like that, she tasted the mold of the dampest parts of the ground, the copper tang of blood that she knew in the instant was from a squirrel in a tree nearest her. She felt the moss beneath her feet start to crackle. And then just as those things entered her consciousness, something covered her mouth and her tongue tasted the moistness of another's and she felt arms around her waist and the beat of a thudding heart against her chest.

And the thirst was gone.

Yenic pulled his lips from hers and searched her eyes. She took a deep breath, watched him do the same. She could only give the barest of nods.

He took her hand and turned to face Edulph. "We'll go with you."

Edulph nodded, and he let go of Aedus's arm. But Alaysha noticed he licked his lips, and that when he noticed no moisture could soften their cracked surface, he sent an inspecting glance around the rest of his party. One or two of the men reached for their water skins and couldn't conceal their surprise when they found them empty.

Aedus pulled her burnt hand close and cradled it against her chest. Alaysha expected to hear her whimper, but she made no sound.

Yenic stepped towards her before Alaysha could. "Someone bandage her," he said to no one and Alaysha rushed to beat any who thought to fulfill the task. She needn't have bothered: nobody had taken the steps, instead the shadows that had emerged, crossed into the light of the clearing and followed into the woods behind Edulph's retreating back.

"Are you all right?" Alaysha reached out for the girl, and Aedus let go a sob. "Tell me Aedus, are you all right?" She had to kneel to look into the girl's eyes.

"She could have been worse," Yenic said from behind her.

Alaysha looked back over her shoulder. "What do you mean?" He sounded as though he was scolding her, not blaming Edulph.

"I mean you could have killed her."

"I would never—"

"Not intentionally."

It struck her that yes, she would indeed have killed Aedus. She would have annihilated everyone within a leagua, including Barruch, and Yenic. All unintentionally.

"As long as they have her, she is not safe." Yenic said. "Not from them or from you."

Alaysha nodded.

"Unless you can walk away from her, leave her to the mercy of her brother."

"He shouldn't have to be inclined toward mercy for his own sister."

"And yet it would seem that's not the case."

Alaysha touched the top of the head that was burrowed and whimpering into her chest. "No. It would seem he is not as loving a brother as she is a sister."

"So can you leave her?"

"No."

"Then it would seem you are going to war."

Chapter 10

At first, Alaysha thought she could merely wait until an opportune moment to steal away. She and Yenic tried hanging back in the riding queue; Yenic behind her on Barruch's back as they left the oasis and headed toward Sarum, but Aedus had been slung over a beast and tied to a pommel, and she wasn't remotely close enough to rescue. The second plan was to wait for nightfall and attempt rescue then.

That was when Alaysha realized how right Aedus had been about the power of the dreamer's worm.

They were sitting a way off from the fire pit when darkness set in the first night. Neither of them spoke to each other, both lost in their own thoughts. Alaysha watched Edulph's men as they lumbered about with gourds full of ale. She thought it was the perfect opportunity. Aedus sat next to the fire, her owlish eyes alight in the roaring blaze. She couldn't have been more than a few second's dash from them.

But for the squat, barrel-chested men next to her, Aedus was unguarded. And that guard seemed more bent on trying to catch the attention of the only woman in the group. She too was short, but broad shouldered with a tangle of mucked hair that could have been blonde or black when clean. Alaysha supposed it hadn't been clean for months.

They seemed the perfect pair to Alaysha. She decided to tell Yenic that they should become matchmakers.

And then she saw, and was reminded of the power of the dreamer's worm—even a full day since application and rinsing off.

"What?" he asked her when he caught her staring.

She shook her head, changing her mind. Best he not know, she supposed. She felt his hand against her back. "Are you cold?"

She tried not to let the green stripes mesmerize her. They danced in the dark as he moved his head, and the darker it became, the more they glowed.

The man next to Aedus let out a bellow of a guffaw. He pointed across the fire at Yenic.

"He's got Meroshi's curse," the filthy warrior shouted. "Look. He's been marked. Greetha, look," he said to the woman and she stood from her spot a few feet away to peer at Yenic.

"Are you mad?" she asked Yenic and laughed. "Do you see night terrors, little man?"

By then everyone was staring. Even Edulph had found a spot next to the fire to gape and laugh. He lifted his gourd in Yenic's direction. "Long live Meroshi's magic," he shouted and everyone with a gourd of ale lifted it and chorused the cheer.

Alaysha wouldn't look at Yenic, trying to save him the shame. Instead she reached for his hand, but he brushed it away and bolted to his feet.

"You think this is magic?" He made a good show of sounding unaffected, but Alaysha could hear something different in his voice. She tried to catch his eye and failed.

He laughed. "You have no idea about magic." He moved toward the fire and it leapt brighter with each step. No one but her seemed to notice the new light to the fire, the radiance of the new heat.

Greetha eased herself up and threaded her way around the blaze and reached out to touch Yenic's face. She was murmuring to herself as she traced the marks. Alaysha could see Yenic stiffen, bracing himself for her touch even as the barrel-chested warrior on the other side braced from anger. He jumped to his feet, hands clenching and unclenching.

"Leave the pup be, Greetha," he shouted. "What would you want with a fool who gets tricked by Meroshi's magic?"

"I think he's pretty, Spate," she said back and looked into Yenic's face. "He has fire behind his eyes."

This infuriated Spate even more, and had several of the men laughing and mocking the thrown-over lover. Yenic seemed to realize the potential for distraction, same as Alaysha had. Without even a word or glance in her direction, she knew he was going to press the issue until Alaysha could sneak away. She was ready, waiting for the opportunity.

Yenic took Greetha's hand and pulled it to the soft spot at the base of his hairline. A quick surge of jealousy fired through Alaysha when she saw Yenic slip his hand onto the woman's back. He murmured in a language Alaysha didn't understand, but in a tone she recognized. Greetha's fingers went to Yenic's ribcage, tracing the tattaus, trailing down the ink line to his hip. Alaysha's mental fingers went with hers as they moved, and she had to fight to keep the envy from tightening her throat. She knew the feel of that skin, how heated it was, how each muscle met the other with the sharpness of a steel blade. She had to pull her gaze away from Yenic and Greetha, seek out Aedus, nod toward the darkness and hope the girl understood.

Then Yenic declared to Greetha in a voice that lifted to the trees that even a pup was better for a bitch than a pig.

It all fell to chaos after that, and Alaysha took the chance to melt into the darkness.

She could hear the arguing, could hear Greetha's taunting, using Yenic as bait to instigate further fury in her spurned lover. Alaysha tried to block it out as she eased her way through the darkness, around the horses, past a few unconscious men.

She heard the clang of metal on metal and supposed the pig had taken enough taunts. She didn't care. She only cared that she get to Aedus. She imagined Yenic could take care of himself. She thought of him letting Greetha's touch and thought it would serve him right anyway.

She glanced at the fire from the shadows, hoping to catch Aedus's eye, hoping even against hope that she had slipped away. Her space was empty. She must be close.

"Aedus sends her regrets," a voice drawled.

Alaysha had been so intent on the fire she hadn't noticed the shadows next to her were too thick. She turned to face Edulph.

"I have a few regrets of my own."

She felt him shift in the darkness, and he was closer to her than she expected. She could smell the oil and mud in his hair, hear the rustling of his beard as he ran his palm down his chin. If he could be measured by his voice alone, it would be pleasant; a person might think him agreeable.

"I've honored my promise," he said.

She felt his breath on her shoulder and rubbed her arm where it touched.

"You mean you haven't held her other hand over the flame"

"To what end would that be useful? You're here with us. We'll be in Sarum in three days, maybe less."

"And so long as I cooperate, she will be fine."

He said nothing for a long while; Alaysha wanted to press his answer, but she knew better. Finally, he spoke again and his tone was harsher than before, more business like.

"Your man has power like you?"

She wasn't sure how to answer that: make him fear or make him wonder? Alaysha said nothing, just turned on her heel and found her way back to the fire, Edulph's annoying chuckle following.

By the time Yenic saw her, Greetha had already found a more accommodating companion than either Spate or Yenic. Several men nursed cuts and a few were clapping Spate on the back.

Yenic sported a good-sized cut on his cheek. He looked at Alaysha and shrugged. "Couldn't let him lose," is all he said, but there was fire still behind his gaze and he glared at Spate as he sat down.

That fire stayed in his eyes for the next two days and even as the glow dissipated, no one in the crew forgot he'd been marked. Each night, Spate found a way to challenge him; each night Yenic suffered through it. Alaysha could see the tension building around the fire.

"What are we going to do?"

"I think we have two choices: we could follow Edulph to Sarum and pray the war he plans to bring causes so much commotion we can steal away with her—"

"Or?" That plan didn't seem very likely, and Alaysha had the uncomfortable image of Edulph doing harm to the girl and forcing Alaysha to use her power. There really seemed no way around it.

"Or we just leave."

"You asked me to do that before, back at the oasis," Alaysha said. "I won't do it."

Yenic lifted a gourd of water to his mouth. One thing they hadn't lacked since joining the rogue tribe was food and drink; they had been fed and watered twice just in the first day. Alaysha didn't want to think about where it might have come from. She glimpsed a few desiccated hands hanging from saddles, the odd cloak made of linen rather than the traditional fur. She guessed they looted and killed in every village they came across, adding the violent outcasts from each to their ragged number.

"I wonder what he promised them to keep them in such good order," she mused aloud.

"Who knows," Yenic said, stretching his legs so the soles of his bare feet reached the fire. Three days slow travel, and she could still see the faint green phosphorescent gleam beneath his eyes; but she wouldn't mention it.

"Do you think Edulph will ever let her go?"

He shrugged. "Would you?"

She gave it consideration and didn't like where her mind went. "I can't keep killing."

"Well, you do make a pretty good threat just by your existence."

"But he'd never be able to know if I would turn on him or not."

"Exactly why you shouldn't have let him know you cared for her. Now she'll never be safe and you will never be free."

"Should I have killed them all in the oasis, is that what you're saying? Because if you are, remember you're the one who stopped me." Her face burned just thinking about how he'd accomplished it.

"I stopped you because I didn't want him to see your full power. Better he believes in it but doesn't yet have evidence. That's why it's taking so long to get to Sarum. I bet Edulph is trying to decide if you're real or not."

"And in the meantime, he won't release Aedus."

"Every day we stay with them proves to him how much you care. She is his weapon against you."

Alaysha thought it over. "So, if we just left?"

"Aedus loses her usefulness."

"He might kill her."

"Yes."

"And you would have us take a chance."

"My duty is to protect the witch. Even if it's from herself."

"I don't need protection."

He said nothing to that, merely took another drink and eased back onto his elbows, face lifted to the night sky. She thought he might say something, as though he needed to unburden himself, but he kept quiet for a long time. She finally had to prod him to speak.

"Maybe you are powerful," he answered. "But you are also young and you are untrained."

She doubted this was what was on his mind, but at least he was speaking again.

"Does that bother you?"

There was a shrug in his tone. "We hoped your nohma would train you to control your power."

"She couldn't. She's been gone these last dozen seasons."

He nodded. "Yes. And you went on killing."

She felt a niggle of shame but pushed it away. A warrior did not feel shame either. "Then why didn't you come for me?"

"We tried." He looked at her. "Plenty of times. We came for you through other villages, but you always arrived with your father and took them. We had to wait until you were old enough to begin to question your father's ways for yourself. We didn't think he'd use you to decimate the whole tribe. And when we did realize, it was too late. The oasis was the best we could do. It was our last stand."

Alaysha thought back to the mud hut and the strangeness of the smoke inside. "Magic," she murmured.

"Our own brand, yes. Those crones you saw, they were the others. They used the last of their powers to protect me. Now they're gone."

He shifted so he was closer to Alaysha, his hip next to hers. The crackle of the fire was the only sound for a while as she ran all he'd said through her mind. That she'd been wanted enough to be searched for. That there were others like her.

Yet the things her father said also echoed through her mind. These people were her people—were they like Edulph and his band, bent on selfish chaos? They might be her mother's people, but that didn't mean she wanted any part of them. She'd struck out on her own, and she meant to be on her own.

"Barruch and I will have gone before dawn," she said finally. "If what you say about Aedus being useless is true, then I'll show them I don't care."

"Good choice," he said. "We'll let the fire go down now so they're uncertain of when we left."

"Not us," she said. "Me."

"You'd go without an Arm?"

She got up and went to her horse, where her blade was, where her fur was tucked into the basket, where her tinder bundle was. "This is my arm," she said, hoisting the blade. "And these are my legs." She patted Barruch's rump. "I've needed nothing but these for years."

He shook his head. "You're young. You need training."

"If it's as you say, the only thing I care about will be safe when I leave."

"You care about only one?" he asked and she had to look away so she could lie easier.

"I can't afford to care about much else. Yuri has been right all these years. My only protection from myself or anyone else is to care for nothing." She kissed Barruch between his eyes and pulled her fur from his basket, thinking that even though she wouldn't sleep, she could pretend, and then she could slip away before dawn.

Chapter 11

She planned to leave as soon as Yenic fell asleep, but he sat by the fire for hours. Contrary to his initial plan, he didn't let the fire die down at all. She didn't see him feed it, necessarily, but she knew he must have, off and on through the night, because every so often it would blaze brightly.

Twice, she realized she'd fallen asleep and felt herself jerk awake. Each time, she peered beneath Barruch's legs at the fire and the slumped form beside it, waiting to see if it moved or stayed still. Both times, within moments an arm reached out toward the flame seeking warmth.

So he wasn't going to let her creep away after all.

She got up and quietly packed her things plus the provisions she'd tied into her basket before they'd had left the oasis: a comb of honey wrapped in leaves and tucked into a pouch, a few peaches, and the last of the frog legs they'd roasted. She tucked her fur beneath Barruch's saddle and clucked at him to move. She planned to lead him out of camp then climb on and ride as fast as she could. With any luck, she could be far enough they'd only catch up when she was out of range of harming Aedus.

They could send all the scouts they wanted then. A few scouts she could handle.

She had Barruch's reins in her hand when Yenic crept up to her. She felt him close enough in the dark that she could touch him if she wanted.

"I'll try to get her away," he said to her and she nodded even though she knew he'd not see it.

"Only when it's safe," she said. "And only if they decide she has no use after all."

"It's the best chance for her."

She did reach for him then, and his hand found hers. She found comfort in his touch. "I know," she told him. "But if my leaving doesn't do what we hope for, try to get her away from Edulph. Brother or no, I don't trust him."

Yenic squeezed her hand. She looked back towards their fire only to see it had gone much dimmer.

"Don't worry," he said, following her gaze. "I put dirt on it. There's nothing like a bit of earth to temper a flame."

"Or water," she said.

"Or water." The hand that had been in hers moved to her chin and rested there. "If this works, I'll bring Aedus to the oasis. We'll wait for you."

"I don't know how far I need to go before it's safe."

"It's all right. We have enough there to keep us fed and watered until you do come."

"What if I don't?" She stepped away from him. "Come to you, I mean."

His soft chuckle moved through the darkness. "Oh, you'll return eventually."

"You can't know that."

"But I do."

She felt him reach out for her again, and the warmth of his palm on her lower back surprised her. Before she could stop him, he had pulled her close and placed his mouth on hers. It brought all the heat of his kiss from the oasis to mind, and she felt as though her throat was on fire.

"We're bonded. You won't be able to help yourself."

He stepped away to mince back toward the tempered fire. Curiosity urged her to follow him and find out what he meant, but reason won out and she pressed herself through the bushes, pulling Barruch along behind her.

By mid afternoon Barruch had taken her halfway to the oasis. In the light of day, things seemed far more fixable. On his back, with her hair being taken by the breeze, and the rhythm of his gallop, Alaysha could clear her mind and focus. So much had changed in the quarter turn of the moon, so much had shifted. In these seven turns, she had learned more about her life than in the eighteen seasons she'd lived. To discover her nohma, a woman far too young to be a grandmother, had actually been her aunt made sense. She'd always felt close to Nohma—she just always believed it was because the woman was the only replacement for a mother she'd had. Now she knew the truth, and the truth seemed to be a strange jumble of information that melded between Yuri's story and Yenic's.

Now she had a foster sister. One who was in danger. Every instinct told Alaysha to stay and fight for the girl, but she knew to do so would put her in even greater risk.

She didn't care if her father's tribe was a target. They'd no doubt make short work of Edulph's rogue band if they did attempt an attack alone. All the more reason for Alaysha to run; better she not tempt her father with her power. She wouldn't let herself be used as any man's blade ever again.

If only she had the ability to control it completely, she'd not have nearly so much to worry her. In fact, if she could control the thirst, she'd immediately cease to be useful as another man's weapon. And it seemed the only link to her being able to do so, she'd left with that decrepit group of villains.

"Bonded," she shouted to Barruch, just so she could hear her voice over the thunder of his hooves. "What could he mean?" In her father's tribe the word bond meant to vow allegiance. It meant above all others; a warrior would choose an emir to die for. She'd never sworn a bond oath to her father or any other.

She let Barruch slow when she smelled water. He would need to drink and rest; she'd ridden him harder than she'd expected, and in truth, she needed food. The peaches in her pack were probably bruised by now, but that would just make them all the sweeter.

She left off when they came in sight of the stream they'd stop at a day earlier on their way to Sarum. They'd filled their leather sacks there, and then drunk from them the rest of the days when the water within was musky and hot.

The stream was refreshingly cool. She pulled off her tunic and splashed into the water, letting Barruch, who was more finicky, sample his refreshment from the edge. She would be cold for a while when she got out, but she'd be clean and the smell of cowardice would be well behind her.

She hitched herself up on the bank so she could semi-float, semi-recline without the current taking her far. She looked up into the filigree of branches and leaves that made the encroaching dusk even gloomier. The moon brooded on the horizon of treetops, waiting for the sun to blink out and give night its rule.

She supposed she could set up camp right here. There was a mound of earth covered in thatch and dead brush that she could crouch against. Her back would be protected while she slept, and to her front any encroaching enemies would have to splash through water to get to her. It was a forceful enough current she doubted anyone would try at night. That left her sides exposed, but Barruch would nicker and nudge her if he smelled anyone strange.

She eased up out of the water and pulled her fur from beneath Barruch's saddle so she could wrap in it while it was still warm. It smelled of animal sweat but she didn't care; it stopped her shivering.

Upon inspection, the area proved better equipped for an overnight stay than she'd originally thought. Tinder from dead branches littered the ground and stream bank. Probably from trees that drowned when heavy rains came and covered a few feet of their trunks with stream water. Moss too, was abundant, making her tinder bundle catch easily on the bits of scavenged brambles.

Before long, she was sitting in front of a roaring flame, peach juice gathering on her chin, wrapped cozily in her animal fur while the darkness came alive with the sounds of courting frogs.

Except that she missed Aedus and Yenic, she had never felt so content.

"I hope you enjoyed your peach, old man," she said to Barruch, who had begun to break wind in a noisy manner. She resolved not to ever feed him another, even if she found a cache of them.

She knew the oasis had enough on that one tree to fill her basket three times over, and she knew she was mere hours away from reaching it. Something kept her from going there, though. She wasn't even sure if she would stop there tomorrow. The way Yenic had looked at her; certain. The way he'd said they were bonded. Her belly squirmed in a pleasant way and that made her made her feel confused and anxious. She felt such longing that she couldn't identify it until she found herself reliving the way his lips felt against hers and the way she felt her heart tremor madly when it beat next to his.

Better she stay away for a while.

He knew more about her than she knew herself, and that was disconcerting. If he did manage to get Aedus away safely, and find his way back to the oasis, what would happen if no one was waiting?

Aedus would be out of danger—there'd be no reason for her brother to use her. Yenic would probably even take care of her. They'd wait for a while for Alaysha to arrive, but eventually they would have to realize she wasn't coming and head for other ground. The weather would come, and even if the crones had magicked the place safe, they couldn't possibly protect it from snow and hail.

And what of her and Barruch? She knew her father would send Drahl after her, hoping to talk her into returning. He'd die in the attempt, of course, no matter how many men he had with him. They couldn't take her by force, and her father knew by now that she cared about nothing enough to coerce her.

Except for Aedus. But they didn't know about Aedus. No one in camp would have paid any attention to whether or not the witch had a companion. Bodicca wouldn't have seen the girl slinking around the fire, nor would the other warrior guards.

And then she remembered her father did know. He'd even told Alaysha to take the little ferret with her. He might not have guessed they'd grown close, but he would know their first stop would be the oasis where her last battle had been laid.

And he could have Drahl there now, waiting. Yuri knew as much as Yenic. Maybe more, and he was not afraid of her. He knew her weakness, he said.

She assumed it was caring for someone, but what if it was something else?

The night didn't seem so cozy anymore. She shifted within the fur and found no matter how she sat, she couldn't get comfortable.

She tried to run her memory, letting her thoughts slip back through the last days to her final meeting with Yuri.

She tried to conjure him in her mind, get a feel for the way he looked, and sat, and ate. She could smell again the fragrance of honey and roasted hare, taste the rain that fell when she left his tent, but she couldn't focus enough to bring it all clear.

She was too mixed up with the worry over Yenic and Aedus, the memory of his mouth on hers, the way he sounded when he told her to think of her nohma.

She was staring out into the darkness, letting all those images play in her mind, feeling the heat of the fire on her cheeks as it rose higher and blazed brighter, watching the fireflies play with each other through the trees.

Except those fireflies were moving in unison. Except those fireflies were far too large to be a mating pair. Why wasn't Barruch alerting her, knowing a stranger had entered his camp.

"Alaysha?"

The voice was too familiar for her to question who it was. Her heart leapt and then thudded hard down to her stomach.

Something was wrong.

"Yenic."

He came out of the shadows, stumbling awkwardly, feeling his way forward with his feet, his hands hanging down at his sides. Laden, she thought, with sacks: maybe filled with fruit or foodstuffs. At least she hoped so.

"What have you brought?" It was a cautious question, the niggling feeling in the back of her neck that it was something more, something she didn't want to know, creeping to her hairline. She had a terrible feeling he was carrying pieces of Aedus back to be buried.

"What is it? Why are you green again?" She was standing, though she couldn't remember getting to her feet. Barruch shuffled away, loathe, it seemed, to let Yenic near him.

He managed to make his way into the light of the fire and Alaysha could see what he carried—what he had been carrying for what must have been a very long trek on foot. She tried to do the figuring: one hour on horseback for three on foot, tried to assess how long she'd been there, how far she'd come and how far he'd had to walk. But she couldn't make her mind move past his burden.

They were dangling by their hair from his fingers like sacks, all three: two in one hand, one in the other. They all were bloody and ragged looking as though they had been hacked at with an untempered blade. Their eyes stared forward, mouths gaping. But for one. His mouth was closed.

"Who were they?"

Yenic stared ahead as though he wasn't seeing. With effort, he lifted his load, biceps trembling from the weight. At that height, able to catch the fire light, Alaysha could see he wasn't actually holding them by their hair, but by the rope coiled around each wrist that his fingers were tangled within. Yenic's fingers grasped at the rope to keep some of the dead weight from cutting into his circulation.

"What happened?" She dropped the fur and rushed to help him. She led him closer to the fire. "Sit," she said, easing him onto the ground. She tried to untangle the head whose mouth was shut, but Yenic pulled away from her. Instead he thrust his other hand forward.

It was too tangled in the ropes and hair to get free without her blade. She had to get up and pull her tiny dirk from its pouch. "This'll do," she told him and with an awkward motion tried to saw her way through the ropes. It took some doing, but soon she had his first hand and wrist free. She was making for the other when he stopped her.

"No."

"Why not?"

"I'll do it." He took the knife from her and felt with his fingers for the ropes. Easing the blade beneath like a blind man would skewer his meat, he worked at it, taking great care to gingerly cut through the lashing.

The head made a sickening thud when it met the earth.

Alaysha tried her best to swallow the bile that rose. She wouldn't ask about Aedus. If she didn't ask, she wouldn't have to hear.

"Who were these men?" she asked instead.

Yenic chuckled in a way that made her skin crawl. "Don't you recognize them?" He kicked at one of the heads to his left. "This was the one Aedus was bound to on horseback."

"And this one," he said, nodding at the other, "this one was Edulph's cousin."

"You killed them?"

He laughed. "I tried. It's tough even for a Witch's Arm to kill without a weapon." He winced as he moved.

She studied him closer and saw he was bleeding, that his rib cage looked swollen, that beneath the green around his eyes, he was bruised purple and the swelling of his lids was obscenely close to shutting off all his vision.

"You're hurt."

"So were they before they were dead."

Alaysha looked at the final head. "And this one?"

He flopped over, his head between his knees, and took a few deep breaths before he lifted it up to look at her. "Spate."

She saw it now. The ugly man who loved Greetha.

"They were all close to Edulph. You saw them laugh together. They became lax once they saw you had gone, Aedus wasn't ill treated. I thought I could easily steal her away."

"And?"

He crossed his arms on his knees. "And when I tried, these three opposed me. I thought I was winning."

"Until?"

"Until Edulph shouted at me. He had Aedus by the hand. Even then, I thought at worst he'd get his lackeys to tie me up. I wasn't expecting what he did do."

The niggling feeling made Alaysha's jaw clench. "Yes?"

He reached for the third head and pried open the mouth. His fingers slipped in and extracted a long, phosphorescent length of flesh. It took a few seconds for Alaysha to realize it was a finger.

"Edulph said each day you delay, he will take another. Tonight can be marked as the first day. These men—" he kicked at the head housing Aedus's index finger. "These men were punished for not fighting well enough. They were tied to me to slow me down."

He put his hand on Alaysha's shoulder, and only then did she realize she was trembling and mostly because she realized the true depth of Edulph's nature. He wanted her to do his bidding, but he couldn't resist trying to make that difficult: and all so he could do further harm.

Yenic held her gaze, and Alaysha wasn't sure what she saw in the depths of his amber eyes. "Aedus is not, nor will she ever be, safe with her brother."

She turned her attention to the lumps of flesh so she wouldn't have to look at Yenic anymore. She knew his eyes were by now burning, that the swelling was keeping him from seeing clearly, that soon the only sight he would have would be terrors from his imagination. She quietly got up and dipped water from the stream, and returned to wash his eyes, hoping the coolness would ease the stinging. If Aedus was telling the truth, she might be able to wash away some of the effects, but the green would stay for days.

He sighed each time she ran cool water over his face. And when the bowl was empty, she would get up and refill it, and return to him to pour more across his eyes.

"You know it's her?"

"Who do you think marked me?" His voice was pained.

She reached out for him, so they could connect in some way that would ease the hurt she felt. He took her hand and they sat together silently for a while.

"I didn't know," he said. "I didn't think."

"I know."

"I shouldn't have counseled you so."

"It's not your fault." She was saying to him, but Alaysha wasn't entirely sure she wasn't trying to tell herself the same thing.

"He's more dangerous than we thought, Alaysha. He's not simply out for revenge. He's lost his mind, and what he has left of it has no humanity." She got up and wrapped the fur around his shoulders, the kind of act a mother would do for a sick child. Or a lover.

"Where you going?"

"Where do you think?" She trudged over to Barruch and started saddling him. She'd leave the tinder bundle, the food.

"You're not leaving me again."

She glanced over at him. "You'll be of no use the way you are."

She could see his anger from where she stood. With some effort, he found his feet. "You're young," he said. "You're making an unwise decision."

"Young? You keep saying that. What kind of decision did you make? I listened to you and look where it got Aedus." She choked on the last words because she knew they weren't fair, and had to clamp her mouth shut so she wouldn't cry. She didn't care that her words stopped him dead.

"I say you're young because you are. You need training yet."

"Then teach me. But teach me while we ride. Aedus will not lose another finger."

He nodded and gathered what he could of their provisions. He picked up the phosphorescent digit and tucked it into Barruch's basket. The heads, he kicked into the bushes for the wild cats or dogs.

"I don't have the knowledge to show you much." He climbed up onto Barruch with her help, wincing as he settled. "But I can tell you one thing."

She gathered the reins and kicked Barruch into slow, plodding movements around the fallen logs and bracken. "And that is?"

"You can stop the power from accelerating by refocusing on someone you love."

"That's it?"

"There's more, but it can be that simple when you have nothing else. It's about balance."

She grunted and braced herself for a flat out gallop. They didn't have time, but at least she had a tool. She needed at least that.

Chapter 12

It must have been a painfully horrific ride for Yenic, and yet he slept. Alaysha could feel his head bounce against her back. She grabbed his arms and pulled them tight against her waist, holding them with one hand so he wouldn't fall. His body against hers felt fevered and while the heat felt good, she knew it also meant she'd have to look out for him when they reached Edulph's camp. She wasn't sure how he managed to reach her but to do so would have taken all his energy reserves. Laden with the heavy baggage and on foot, ravaged by battle, she wondered how he was even alive.

In truth, she wasn't sure he would stay so. But she didn't want to think about that. She was losing all perspective. All complacency. She pulled him closer and told herself she shouldn't care about not caring.

She couldn't ride Barruch for hours without resting and watering him, but she pushed the beast farther than she normally would, pulling Yenic down and easing him onto the fur after only a couple of hours. She knew they were close to Edulph's camp. She recognized the terrain.

Barruch was sweating. Yenic was sweating. Alaysha's tunic was wet with perspiration. Thank the Deities she hadn't ridden all the way to the oasis. She looked up at the sky. Dawn was coming and she could easily rest for an hour and still slip into the camp by midmorning.

"Rest, old man," she told Barruch. She stripped off her tunic and used it to wipe him down, and then set about gathering fern tops and sweet grass so he could eat without using the energy it took to forage. She needed him as fresh as he could get in a few hours.

She pulled the stinking leather back down over her head and considered making a fire, then realized she was too tired. Yenic lay on the grass beside Barruch, wrapped in the fur. A few hours. No more. Surely she could catch some sleep. Maybe Yenic would feel better after an uninterrupted rest. She hoped so. Looking down at him, she thought she wasn't sure what she'd do if he didn't make it.

She climbed in next to him. His arm went around her, pulling her close. Nestled there, his heated body next to hers, she was asleep in moments.

Once during the night, Alaysha felt shaken awake. It was deep into the night, so dark, even the shadows slept. She peered groggily into the pit of black and tried to orient herself. Even as she was registering that she slept at the bank of a river and that Barruch was snoring somewhere to her left, she felt the tremors again.

Yenic.

She reached for him and touched fire. Her hand came away so wet and clammy, she was surprised when his irregular breathing felt hot and then deathly cold in between.

She knew if she didn't cool him down, he wouldn't live the night. He might not even live the next few moments.

All she could think to do was run with her bowl and water skin to the stream. In her haste, she'd forgotten how close the river was and she fumbled blindly for a few moments before splashing in and feeling the shock of cold. Close, so close. And not yet close enough. She wouldn't be able to keep him cool enough by running back and forth, filling and refilling her bowl.

She dipped both vessels in together and had to guess about how much it would take to fill the skin. A few splashings later and she was on the bank, plodding, nearly blind in the direction she thought her mat waited.

She stubbed her bare toe and cursed. Where was her mat, anyway? Her eyes stung from pain and trying to squint into the shadows. She'd obviously gone in the wrong direction. A low snort came from her right hand. Barruch. "Good boy," she said to the sound.

She waited, poised to sprint. Another low snort and whinny, closer this time.

She smelled horseflesh and reached out, holding the water skin aloft. Barruch's nose ran along her wrist, and she felt the heat of his breath. He turned and Alaysha took careful steps with him. Best to stay calm. Her concern for Yenic was working against her, not helping. Stay calm. Stay focused. One step. Two.

Barruch stopped after a dozen paces. Alaysha peered into the darkness and thought she saw a rounded blacker-than-the-darkness mound.

She rushed to it, hoping she was right, and placed the water down next to what she thought was Yenic's head.

She fumbled for him. The heat came at her in waves before she even touched the skin of his face.

"Yenic," she said.

He moaned and relief flooded her; at least he was alive. She couldn't afford to waste any time. She knew the small amount of water she carried wouldn't be enough. He needed to be bathed in it, submerged. There was only one thing she could think to do.

"I'm sorry," she told him, then grasped him as gently as she could beneath the shoulders. Like she'd done to the crones in the village, she buck-dragged him toward where the water smelled strongest. The sound of the current grew louder with each yank, and she began to believe she could manage it.

The spasms took him when she was at least one hard pull away. The spasm felt different than before. It straightened his legs and stiffened his shoulders. She let go of him and reached for his chest. Her palm rested on his solar plexus, waited impatiently for a rise and fall, for a thump beneath.

Nothing.

Her palm hovered over his mouth, and she waited for a rush of air.

None.

Her finger scrabbled for his throat just behind his earlobe.

A flutter, but not much after it except for a thready, cautious trembling.

She reached for his mouth and pulled his mouth open, easing her own down over his so that no air could escape. She inhaled through her nose and sent a silent plea to the Deities to fill her lungs with sweet air. She exhaled.

It was nothing like the time his mouth had been on hers before. Back then his lips were moist and warm, pleasant in a heart-stopping way. This time those same lips were dry and hot and frightening in a heart-stopping way. This time there was no pleasure, only steely focus. She breathed in, lifted her mouth from his, waited, breathed in again.

Each time she thought the fire within him would ignite her mouth and lungs. Each time she felt her own air rise in temperature when it met his mouth, but she exhaled anyway, hoping the heat wouldn't burn his lungs.

She was near exhaustion when she thought she felt it: a short, rasp against her cheek. She nearly laughed out loud from relief.

"Yenic?"

A louder breath this time, one she couldn't misinterpret. Thank the Deities.

Now if she could just get him to the water.

She grasped him again, and pulled with all she had left, stepped backwards, yanked again. Stepped again, and felt the gasping coldness of the stream. This time she did laugh.

She let her fingers walk to his legs and pulled them so they could find the water. He slipped easily into the stream then; she could hold his head and torso close to the bank, but leave most of his body in the water, could hear the current fetching against him and complaining. It was the sweetest sound she'd heard in days.

She stroked his hair, feeling over and over again for a pulse at his neck, never quite daring to believe it was getting stronger.

The sun was bleeding onto the horizon when his eyes fluttered open. Only then did she pull him back onto the bank, strip him, and with his help, settle him back into the fur. She worked on a small, but passable fire to keep any chill from devouring his body after the rapid cool down of the stream. After, without a word, she settled next to him.

She tried to be gentle when she shook him awake. Exhausted as she was, she'd slept longer than she'd hoped. In the light of full morning, she realized the full extent of his wounds. Both eyes were swollen and a large gash over his right brow had bled and caked overnight. The tattaus on his ribs were distorted from the swelling. She had an incredible urge to feed him, to touch him, to make him feel better.

"Are you hungry?" She thought she had some frog legs left over.

He shook his head. "Thirsty."

She had a water skin she'd filled from the stream. He drank almost all of it.

"You had quite a battle," she said. She couldn't help the pride in her voice when she said it.

He closed his eyes thoughtfully. "So did they."

"Will Edulph let me be if I agree?"

"I don't know. If you had control of such a weapon as a temptress of the life blood, would you relinquish it?"

Her father hadn't, that much she knew. She shook her head. "Probably not. Not if I were one of his kind."

"So we must make you a less valuable weapon," he said, and tried to ease up onto his elbow but had to be content to study her face from a flat-back position.

"How?"

"There are two ways. One is to become so controlling of the power, no one else can control you. I've known a witch to be able to bring lightening to a man and set stones ablaze."

"I can't do that."

"Of course not; you are a temptress of fluid, not of fire." He tried unsuccessfully to get up again and fell back with a groan.

"Everything is spinning." He peered at her. "And you seem to have two noses. Beautiful as they are, it's unnerving."

"You're going to hurt yourself." She was set to help him, all perched on her elbows, leaning forward.

He let go a raspy chuckle. "Already accomplished."

She thought about his words. "Temptress of fire? Is there such a thing?"

"There are more. Earth. Water. Fire. Air. I told you: balance." He pulled the fur beneath his chin and shivered. Alaysha looked down at him. His fever had broken but wasn't gone entirely. He was in no shape to stay alone; he was in no shape to continue.

"You have to stay here."

"No," he said, but he didn't open his eyes.

"Then follow when you're better." She hated leaving him, but she knew if he'd made it through the worst of last night, he had a good chance—even if it was a long recuperation—of making it through these next days.

"I am better."

She slipped out from beneath the blanket and strode toward Barruch who was munching contentedly on grass. He didn't look pleased at his impending journey. "Not long now, old man," she said. "A couple of hours of riding." She stole a look over her shoulder at Yenic to be sure he was still where she'd left him, then she worked at saddling Barruch.

"You're better than last night, but not better enough to come. Aedus and I will go to Sarum. I will bide my time until we can escape."

"Your father?"

The voice came from so close behind her, she startled. She turned and saw he was standing right there, wrapped in the blanket. He was weaving to and fro and blinking repeatedly. Trying to stay awake, probably.

"My father means nothing to me now. What do I care if one more man dies? One more tribe?"

He collapsed onto the ground, the fur puffing out around him. His words were slurred from fatigue and he kept rubbing his eyes. Once, he peered, transfixed, at a spot somewhere beyond Alaysha. "You'll be trading one master for another, I expect." He squinted into the distance.

She shrugged and untied her scabbard and sword from Barruch's pack, then laid it in easy reach should Yenic need to use it. She gave him a long look, then turned, mounted, and pulled the reins tight. Only then would she speak to his comment.

"It's a temporary enslavement. Once Edulph's guard is down, I'll send Aedus to you."

He seemed to accept that. "Mind the huts; take care those within don't see you."

She looked over her shoulder. There were no huts anywhere near. No people. She shrugged. He must be concerned about her going toward the village near the oasis. He'd want that spot protected—wouldn't want Edulph or his men to know that's where they were headed or where they'd end up meeting for fear they'd come and start the thing all over again.

"I'll be careful."

"What are you going to do, Alaysha?"

She couldn't help the grin stealing her face, or the sense of burning anger that spread it. "I plan to suck them all dry."

Chapter 13

She could tell she was close to the encampment because of the noise. A set-down always owned its share of extraordinary sounds that didn't belong in nature: the low hum of speech, the high-pitch of tempers flaring. Sometimes there was a soft rush of fragrance on the breeze that smelled of new fire and roasted meat. The one thing that gave away a moving camp set down for a short siege was the whine of beasts, and Barruch's ears always perked and twitched at that sound. If Alaysha reached out to test the air for water, she would taste sweat and cooking water in overabundance.

But she didn't need to.

She planned to find Aedus first, to see if she could be squirreled away quietly without Alaysha having to reveal herself. She reckoned she had a few hours until sunset, and she planned to use the time to her advantage. She dismounted and looked around for a good spot to tether Barruch. She had seen a knoll about a half kubit back that had sufficient tree cover. She could walk him back there and hide him by piling branches all around. Perhaps she'd use Aedus's trick of slicking her hair back with mud. Maybe cover herself with it so she'd blend in to the wood cover.

She found a mud hole of considerable size. Left from the last rain, it was dried of liquid, but the hollow left in the land was filled with debris and leaf litter that had rotted there. The combination made a revolting mess that slid easily over her hair, but it also stunk. Barruch backed away from her when she tried to hide him behind tree branches.

The snap of a twig behind her made her jump. Yenic. How had he made it so far in his condition?

I told you to stay put." She turned to scold him. No one was there.

She squinted into the underbrush, searching for a hare or deer. No other sound came. If it was Yenic, he'd have answered. If it was an animal, it would have moved by now.

She stepped closer to Barruch, thinking to pull her sword from its scabbard, and when she did, remembered she'd left it with Yenic. She contented herself with the small dirk she used to cut fruit, and palmed it quickly, the handle set behind her wrist.

The light shifted enough that she could make out a set of eyes in the trees. Then another. Two, she could manage without her power; three, and she wasn't sure she'd have a chance. So much for sneaking into camp. She just hoped they'd not take another of Aedus's fingers for her subterfuge.

"Is this how you've evaded us, Witch?"

Alaysha peered, leaning into the shadows.

The voice was a familiar one. The speaker shifted from shade to shade and finally out into the light.

"You cover yourself with filth to hide in the shadows. Pitiful for a witch, I'd say."

She knew him now, and she knew as soon as she saw him that all chance of freeing Aedus was gone.

She tried to keep her voice level when she spoke. "You've been looking for me?" She asked Drahl. "Why? I thought Father wanted me to find number nineteen." She'd almost said Yenic, but caught herself just in time.

"It's taking too long. He wants to see the eyes and know it's done."

She shrugged, but a flash of insight came so quickly, she was afraid she'd given herself away. "Number nineteen is with this band. Hiding from us within their ranks."

"Then kill them and be done with it." His gaze narrowed, and she thought she saw suspicion behind his eyes.

"I would have, except I thought I saw your property with them as well. I wanted to be sure before I attacked."

"My property?"

"Yes." She tried to watch his face for reaction without appearing to be studying him. "I believe they have someone who belongs to you."

"I have enough slaves." He waved his hand dismissively, "What do I care for one more?"

She turned away from him. "That makes it easy then." She looked back over her shoulder. "You might want to move back a few kubits." She nodded her head at the other set of eyes. "Him too."

Drahl grunted, apparently satisfied she was about to complete the task she'd been sent out on. He inclined his head toward the trees, and three more men slipped out from behind tree trunks.

She took a decided step in the opposite direction of the rogue's camp, praying to the Deities that Drahl would move his men toward the camp. She had no doubt about their reception once the sentries caught sight of them.

"Take yourselves at least a couple of kubits in to be safe."

She took a breath and trudged forward, thinking she'd double back when they were out of sight and in the chaos, she was sure to get to Aedus, sure she'd be left unguarded.

Drahl and his men didn't even bother trying to be quiet, they were so confident the enemy would soon be dead and they'd be well enough away to escape all danger from the witch. She could hear them laughing among themselves, crashing through the thicket. Walking their mounts noisily through the brush.

Good. They'd be noticed. And quickly. That meant she had to hurry. Once she could only hear them from a good distance, she turned to the right and circled. She knew the camp was at the break of the treeline, with sentries posted everywhere in the bushes. The natural sneakiness of a rogue band meant they'd want to disappear quickly and melt into nature. So while they hadn't given consideration to how smart it would be to camp far enough into a clearing that they couldn't be taken by surprise, they at least understood the value of escaping should they be come upon. Or they were just stupid, making the wrong assumption that they were the ones with the advantage.

Twice, she caught an overhanging branch in the face in her haste, and once she stumbled over a root she wasn't watching for. But soon, she was close enough she could almost smell the roasting fire. From her spot in the trees, she could tell the sun hadn't set yet. Still some time before Edulph took the next digit. If she was lucky. Now all she had to do was wait until the sentries either found Drahl, or Drahl walked unawares into the plain.

She crept closer, close enough she could see the fire. The horses were resting, tied to fallen trees. Just under two dozen still, so she knew they were all close to camp.

She crouched behind a large rock trying to see past the horses, to the fire. Luckily, they were a small enough group that they kept together when they camped and didn't sprawl out like an army did. She knew she should be looking to count forty or so bodies in all, including Aedus, but there was no telling how many would be in the trees. Some were hunched, cloaked, around the fire. She could make out three of these in the encroaching gloom. Was one of them Edulph? She couldn't know for sure.

A racket to her left told her Drahl and his party had been spotted. Shouts met her ears, as did the clanging tension of metal in the air. Only the discipline of a dozen battles and hundreds of training sessions let Alaysha keep her attention on the fire.

Several forms lifted from places she'd not noticed: behind trees, crouched next to fallen logs, shadows that were pools on the ground: all lifted, and lighted, grabbing blades and rushing the darkness.

All but one form that no longer crouched at the fire. Aedus. She scrambled, fell, and scrambled again toward the horses, where she fell again and lay still beneath the belly of the largest mount.

Alaysha wasted no time.

She sped into the clearing and threw herself beneath the beast. The feel of the scrawny shoulders beneath her hands was a relief; the frightened eyes peering up at her, a shock.

"You're not Aedus." Alaysha could hear the disappointment in her own voice.

The girl shook her head.

"Aedus is gone."

"Gone?" Alasha had a hard time keeping her voice down or the despair out of it.

"With Edulph."

The skirmish had escalated into a fully fledged battle. Several men had leaked from the treeline into the clearing and the shouts had turned to the low grumble of grunts that came with the effort of battle. Drahl was a scout, not a warrior. He'd not be able to hold his own for long. Soon it would be over and she still hadn't found Aedus.

"Where did they go?"

The girl shook her head. "Into the woods."

She pointed toward where Alaysha had come from.

She grabbed the girl's hand, counted the fingers with her own. Grabbed for the other. All ten were there. She groaned; so it had been Aedus's finger sent with Yenic and not a substitute.

"But why?" Alaysha sat back on her haunches, deflated. It made no sense. Unless he expected her to try and sneak in, but in that case, why not just lay a trap so she wouldn't succeed?

He was far more unpredictable than she'd thought. It seemed he planned to lure her ever closer to Sarum while he made it impossible to get to Aedus, and made Alaysha's desperation to get to her all the more urgent.

She huffed and scanned the trees and plain. There were several bodies on the ground and at least a dozen fights still being fought. Those were tiring, however, and a victor would soon be clear.

She heard a gathering shout from a voice she recognized and knew it was Drahl calling his men to retreat. It was clear the rogues would be too tired to follow and were disinclined to finish them off.

She had to get out of there.

The girl gripped her arm. "Don't leave me here." Her face was white with fear in the dark.

"I can't take you."

Alaysha studied her, thinking. She could quench this entire fire pit of madness within seconds. And the world of Drahl, and of this fighting. She could safely get away to Barruch and be off to free Aedus without worry of being followed.

But this girl would die.

Did that matter?

She would probably die anyway; either from hunger or at the hands of these ruffians.

"Can you ride?"

The girl nodded.

"Then get on a horse and make your way back to the west. A day straight along, maybe a day and a half past a small stream to a place of unusual desert. You'll see a grove of trees. Go there. It's the best I can do." She set to spring off into the undergrowth, hoping she'd not already been seen, when the girl clutched at her arm again.

Alaysah shook her head. "I can't take you."

"They'll catch me."

"What do you matter?" It was blunt, but there wasn't time to play at diplomacy.

"I'm Yuri's daughter."

The bald statement took the air from Alaysha's lungs. She knew her father had children besides her, but except for the tiny heir, she'd not been allowed near any. This girl couldn't be more than eight or nine. Aedus had to be around the same age—maybe a season or two more.

She grabbed the girl by the hand without saying a word to her and pulled her along as she crouched, and ran to the trees.

She couldn't believe her good fortune that they found shelter behind a copse of trees without being noticed. She turned to the girl, knelt in front of her.

"Tell me."

The girl stammered, and worked at her eyes with her palms, but she managed a few words of nearly unintelligible speech. Alaysha had to be patient. She held onto the small shoulders in the darkness and tried to ease the girl's shivering.

"Tell me about Aedus."

"I told you, she's gone."

"Why do they have you? How could they have managed it?"

The girl's shrug stole Alaysha's last ounce of patience.

"You know something. If you're Yuri's daughter you must know why you're here."

She could tell the girl was trying to be brave. She could feel the effort the girl made to stop trembling.

"I was playing. A man slipped out of the bushes. We rode for days from Sarum. That's all I know."

"But you've seen Aedus?"

The girl nodded. "We were kept together for the whole day we were here."

"Was she okay?" Alaysha wasn't sure she could stand the answer.

A voice came from behind her in answer. "She gets less okay each day."

Alaysha froze in her spot. She knew she'd waited too long. Now she was caught. She sensed at least one man behind her. She took her time getting to her feet.

Too bad about the girl, but now that she had her, had met her, she couldn't let her die the same death as these bastards, she'd have to refrain from using the power.

She turned slowly. Yes. Two. She once more thought of the sword she'd left with Yenic, hoping to be fleeter of foot. Now she wished she'd been smarter.

"Tell me about Aedus," she told the men.

The both looked at her and laughed at the same time. One came forward to wrestle the girl from her arms.

"Don't touch her," Alaysha had gone to the trouble of getting her safely away from these men, she wasn't about to give her back to them.

The man didn't back off, but neither did he make a move toward the girl. Alaysha took that as a good sign.

"You were waiting for me," she said.

"Edulph was sure you would come."

"And Aedus?"

"She believes her brother is saving her from us. Stupid girl."

Alaysha looked at the girl—her half-sister—if she could be believed. "Why her? What does she have?"

He snorted. "Questions you should ask Edulph."

"What about Drahl?"

He laughed and his companion slapped his thigh with his palm in warped humor. "That dog? He has slunk back to his den."

He didn't need to say what would happen when he was found. Alaysha sighed. Should Drahl manage to live and return, he would find Alaysha with these people. He would believe, rightly so, that she'd let him walk into a trap. He just wouldn't know why. Had he known about the girl? Surely not, or he wouldn't have ordered their deaths so blithely.

"The girl and I want to sleep by the fire. And we want blankets. And I want a sword. A sharp one."

The sky had turned crimson and the whole campsite looked bathed in blood. She prayed to the Deities they could make it through the night without having to shed any more.

It took a few moments, but the man nodded and shuffled off. He returned when Alaysha and her sister were feeding the fire to make it good and high, it's light casting a few good horse strides in each direction.

She tested the edge of the blade he brought and nodded at him.

"Fine. Now you and your men will sleep beyond where the light rests. If you so much as come within a few steps of it, I will kill you without thought."

He smirked but said nothing. He would test her, she knew that. Maybe him or another, but she would be tested. She hoped she could get through the night without having to use her thirst, but she would use it if she had to. Better the girl died at her hand than be subjected to a horde of callous men.

She spread the bearskin he'd brought as close to the fire as she could and bid the girl crawl beneath it. Then she covered her with the other and sat next to her, sword in hand, facing the fire but painfully aware that her back was unprotected.

"What's your name, girl?"

"Bronwyn."

"Well, Bronwyn, sleep if you can, but if you can't, don't speak to me unless I speak to you first. I need to listen to the night."

There was a short pause, and Alaysha thought her bluntness had hurt the girl, but then her voice came and made Alaysha's eyes sting.

"She was brave," Bronwyn said. "When Edulph took her. She didn't cry at all."

"Thank you," Alaysha whispered.

They came when Alaysha felt the weariness the most. They must have been watching her, waiting for her head to nod, for her shoulders to slump. If she had been cleverer, she would have thought to fake the fatigue while she was still sour enough to add the fury to her fight.

As it was, they got well within the light before she jarred awake, and it took several awkward seconds to get her feet. She swayed once before the adrenaline kicked in and the hesitation gave them the time they needed to bound across the fire.

There were two to begin the attack. The rest, the last seven or eight stood off in the shadows, moving and shuffling there.

The first managed to get close enough to Alaysha that she had to jump back to gain the distance to swing her sword. She had to shout at the girl to find her feet and keep her back as close as she could to Alaysha's.

To her credit, the girl's response was instant and Alaysha could feel the heat of her, dancing with her, sidestepping as she took the measures of the men.

Her mentors had taught her to say nothing when she fought, not to waste a single breath on words. She kept her sword low, but close to conserve the energy it took to hold it aloft. She took long, slow breaths; her skin hummed. She felt the air against the flesh of her eyes, so wide were they, taking in everything she could. She could hear the breathing of the man to her left. It was ragged. Excited. Too sure of his own confidence and the outcome to be even. The other one was measuring his breaths, taking slow inhales like she was.

The one to the left would be dead in seconds; the other would try for her then, she knew. She had to find a way to make both of those things unexpected so the second would not gain from the stupidity of the first. That meant she had to strike and she'd have to strike for the one who was prepared to use his comrade's misfortune to his advantage.

She made no sound, just filled her lungs as best she could and lunged. And swung. And twisted in the circle, prepared to make the loop even if she contacted nothing.

She aimed high. And stepped to the right. The first swing connected with something that caught and held her blade. A stab met pure air. A force struck her legs and rolled her over twice. She barely held onto the hilt, and twisted awkwardly. Hot coppery liquid trailed down her wrist.

So. She'd got the first, but the moron had her on her back. She needed to find her feet or she'd be finished. And the girl would be finished.

She felt a blade against her throat and a clammy hand against the inside of her thigh. "I was glad to see you," he said. "We see so few women."

The blade was so hard against her throat, she could smell her own blood, but she wasn't afraid. She knew he'd lose interest in the knife soon enough. All she had to do was let go the sword where she could grab it again. Let go. Let go. Her fingers finally obeyed her and dropped the hilt noiselessly on the ground. She waited, so patiently, 'til he pressed his hips closer to hers, all his weight going into working at pulling down his breeks.

And she jammed her fingers as hard as she could into his eyes. A scuffling sound came from her left where she'd dropped the blade. She had to get him off her before whoever had the sword could use it.

Too late. She heard the whistling sound of it eating air, and she braced herself to feel it slicing into her.

There was a meaty thunk as his weight went dead on her. Someone in the shadows cursed.

Alaysha pushed at the body atop her and rolled to her side when it fell away. When she gained her feet, she saw Bronwyn standing framed in firelight, the sword hanging at her side, tip pointing to the ground.

"You did good, little one."

Bronwyn nodded, mute. Alaysha took the sword from her. She held it high and shouted at the shadows, watched them disperse.

"Careful, dogs. Yuri's daughters are trained like men to be warriors. You would do well to remember your pitiful lives when next you think they can be used for sport."

She put her hand on the girl's shoulder. "We can sleep now."

The girl gave a lingering look at the blanket. "I don't think I'll ever sleep again."

Chapter 14

Alaysha suffered dreams that seemed more memory than night visions. In them, she traveled like a drop of water through fibres and muscles and tear ducts. She fell as dried fruit from eye sockets of dying men, laid down roots into arid sand and waited for the whispering song of rain. Once or twice she woke to the sounds of wolves snarling, and in her drowsiness told herself they were just after the man Bronwyn had killed—that they'd leave the camp alone.

When she felt the sun on her face and heard squirrels chattering to each other, she got up and woke Bronwyn who had fallen asleep after all.

None of the men spoke to them. She carried the sword in plain sight anyway.

Alaysha had been given plenty to eat when she and Yenic had traveled with them the first time; this last leg of the journey found the stores wanting. The fire provided heat for those rousing before dawn—and Alaysha watched them with wary eyes—even those men who kept their distance but shot her hateful looks. Some of the men eventually came forward with squirrels that they'd skinned and stuck to the ends of sticks. These they poked into the hottest part of the embers, and Alaysha realized then the full extent of the wear on the stores.

If they'd not been so gluttonous, they might have more to eat among them than a few squirrels, snakes, and overripe gooseberries.

She watched a few of them come and go at the fire, some of them throwing in whole, un-skinned snakes, others large hairy spiders that stank when they cooked. Most squatted and leaned in, avoiding her eye. One man, a thin strip of leathered frame with so much hair she thought he could stand to go a night without a cover, came within spitting distance and threw a handful of yellow wriggling things onto a flat rock at the edge.

She immediately perked up.

"You eat those?" she asked him.

He shrugged. "Never did before, but Edulph said to try it."

"They taste like roast boar," she said.

He watched them sizzle against the stone in the juices from the dying bodies. Once, he even grimaced.

"That's not nearly enough to make a meal," she said, trying on a sympathetic tone. Bronwyn was gagging discreetly as she sat next to her.

He met her eye. "Edulph didn't want to waste many if they weren't edible."

"Oh, they're edible." She tried to smile her encouragement. The real truth was she'd left the entire mess for Yenic back at the oasis because they were too disgusting to think about eating, but if Edulph was down to eating his tribe's dreamer's worm, then she knew their food supply was indeed gone. Not great planning for a potential leader. Maybe not such a potential leader, then. She scanned his crew, who were all either rummaging through the bushes, trying to catch and skin squirrels, or beating the bushes for snakes.

Fierce fighters, maybe, but untried in true campaign.

For the first time in days, she felt the stirrings of hope.

The swarthy fellow scraped stiff grubs into a wooden bowl and Alaysha caught him shivering in disgust.

"I can take that to him if you like."

He gave her a patronizing look across the short flame. "Who else do you think was going to bring it?" The man nodded in the direction of two men who stood at the edge of the tree line. "He's just beyond." He grinned and showed a broken front tooth. "And leave the girl."

She pulled Bronwyn close. "I won't leave her alone."

The man whistled and Greetha rose up from a pile of furs. "Watch the girl," he said and Greetha groaned. "Edulph wants to talk to the witch, and I don't think the witch trusts us with her little girl."

Alaysha didn't trust the woman any more than the men. "Here." She passed the sword to Bronwyn. "Don't be afraid to give that one company." She nodded at the remains of the body from the night before lying on the edge of camp.

Bronwyn clenched the sword in white-knuckled hands and only then, did Alaysha make a move toward the trees.

The man grunted at her. "Don't forget his breakfast."

She took the bowl to where the men waited. Without a word, they ushered her past the pines and spruce into a small clearing devoid of vegetation. The needles on the ground softened any noise.

"You're hungry," she said to the lump at the base of the tree. He was wrapped in fur against the early morning chill. Alaysha scanned the clearing for Aedus.

"She's safe."

Alaysha eased the bowl onto the ground at the statement. There was tension in the air that she could taste in the back of her throat, and she wanted her hands free just in case.

"You say she's safe."

"If I say it, it must be true." He unfolded from the blanket and got up. "She tells me you eat these." He stabbed his finger at the bowl.

Alaysha lifted a shoulder. "Some do."

He grunted and for the first time she noticed his fingers were a wriggling mass of yellow. A handful of them in his hand, came from a pile of roiling grubs on the ground next to his fur.

"Someone's been busy."

"There's a pond near my site," he said. "Aedus and I have been fishing."

"But you caught nothing?"

He sighed. "Just these worms; she seemed fairly excited."

"Have you been feeding her?"

"Of course. She's my sister."

Alaysha was tired of the game. "What do you want?"

He slunk forward, dropping the grubs with a pitter-pat to the earth and reached for a lock of her hair that he then trailed across his fingers. He smelled of old sweat and sour dirt. "Feels nice," he said. "If only you weren't ruined by that hideous tattau." He grimaced in pity.

She jerked away and his expression hardened. "Did you like my present?"

"Present? Those severed heads, Aedus's finger, or Yenic's battered body?"

A smile slithered across his face. "All of them were one large gift."

"I liked it as much as I like you."

"Oh, you're harsh, even for a witch. Do you know how you came to receive those heads?"

"I was there, wasn't I?"

"Not for the first of it, the wrapping of the gift, so to speak."

She refused to encourage him by speaking. He stepped away from her, letting a finger trail down her arm. She had to work at not shuddering in revulsion.

"My best men," he said. "Your Yenic shows such promise as a warrior. Spate—he was the first, my good cousin—he caught the traitor stealing up to Aedus in the early hours, after our meal. We had drunk a fair bit, I must say, and it made us all a little off our play."

"So you only thought it fair to pitch him against three?"

He pooched his bottom lip into the top, making it look like a slug had nestled in his beard.

"Wouldn't you think it fair? One drunken man would never be able to hold his own against a sober one. Although, I must admit also, that Spate kept his grog pretty well. Some have even said it made him that much fiercer a fighter."

He settled down against a tree. "Sit," he told her. "You will hear it all."

She didn't want to hear any of it, and yet she wanted more than anything to. She wouldn't move closer, though, and selected a rock with enough moss on it to add comfort, far enough away that she didn't have to concern herself with accidentally touching him.

"So," she said. "Go on."

He smiled then, and leaned forward as though he were telling an exciting tale to a sleepy child. She thought him completely mad.

"Your Yenic had no weapons at all, poor thing. He had to weave and bob like some thief in the marketplace. He's quite skilled in defense, even without a sword—even against one." He smiled, but there was no humor in it.

"Used his body like a battering ram, knocking poor Spate down and crashing his forearms over and over onto his face."

He cocked his head. "I heard his nose break. That's when I knew Spate needed help."

"So you sent the others." She forced her tone to sound unimpressed. "I know this."

"Ah, but do you know your man called for fire?"

She tried not to show interest. "Called for fire?"

"Yes, in the old tongue. The fire pit blazed so bright no one could get near it except your man."

Fire clan, he'd said. He did have an affinity. Alaysha had seen it herself.

"Eventually, my men had to charge through the heat, and they were glistening with the sweat of it—I swear, they looked like their juices were roasting right out of them, but your man never broke a bead."

He looked at her so thoughtfully, almost admirably, that she almost forgot she was conversing with a man who had harmed his own sister.

"I've never seen such a fighter in all my days."

She snorted. "You don't look a day over twenty seasons."

He shrugged. "My thanks to you. But you should know my tribe is taught to fight as soon as the moss is taken from our swaddlings. By the time we're four seasons old, we have contests each year where we're pitted against a fighter two seasons older. We learn to fight or we learn to die."

"And how is it you still live?"

The slug returned to his beard as he chewed the insides of his cheek. "I nearly died. Then I grew smart. And that's why I'm here to tell you. But I'm digressing."

"Your man had no weapon but for the things he found: rocks, tree branches, hot stones from the fire, once even a dead rat he'd somehow come upon." Edulph stared out into the woods as though he was reliving it. "It wasn't clumsy either. It was something almost magical, the way he used his body, how he intercepted their swings."

"Swings? They had swords?"

Edulph snapped back. "Oh, yes. You don't think I'd send my men to battle unarmed?"

Alaysha tried to imagine it and couldn't. Yenic had been beaten and bruised and cut up. She realized then that perhaps he was so battered because his body was the only weapon he had.

"So, how did they come to be the ones who lost their heads?"

He lifted a wiry shoulder. "They weren't winning, so I called them off and sent for Aedus."

"You took her finger, then, didn't you? Because you knew Yenic wouldn't stop fighting for her."

He nodded almost happily. "Worked like any magic I'd ever imagined. Even better. Your man became quite docile then."

"And you killed your men."

He raised a finger in objection. "I delegated their killing. Then I had Greetha ride your man out of camp and dump him."

"How thoughtful."

"Well, we did want him to get to you... eventually. Strong as he is, I doubt he would have made it the whole way in his condition."

She could barely believe what she was hearing. "So why are you telling me this?"

He chuckled. "I tell you all this to tell you this:

"With all his strength and determination, your man still wasn't able to best me. No. In the end, I beat him. I outsmarted him. I out-strategized him."

He pinned her with a stare that didn't move from hers. "You see, not all battles are about physical strength. And if strength isn't enough and it's the last best thing you have, and yet your opponent spares no one the blade—not even beloved warriors or sisters, how do you think you can win?"

He waved his hand in dismissal. "Now go. Collect up your little sister and settle yourself to do what is asked of you and remember who is leading this battle."

She stomped out of the clearing unmolested and with his braying laugher at her back.

She glared at anyone who looked at her and selected a horse to share with Bronwyn. There was no use in hoping Barruch was still at his post. Drahl would have collected him. She hoped he'd be in Sarum when she got there. She reached down to help the girl up.

"Aren't you hungry?" The girl offered Alaysha a burnt piece of squirrel.

"I'll eat when this is over. I don't want to spend any more time with these men than I have to."

Bronwyn murmured agreement and settled in front. Alaysha felt the warmth of her back and the weight of her head.

"Last night you told the man Yuri's daughters were warriors."

"I did."

"Are you, too, Yuri's daughter?"

"I am."

"From which mother?"

"My mother is dead."

Bronwyn went quiet for a moment. "Mine too," she said after a while.

"I'm sorry."

"It's okay. I have many sisters, but only one brother."

"The young babe?"

"Yes. But he won't live the season."

This was news. "Why not?"

"The witch made him ill. He couldn't drink, so the guardsmen say, and when his mother could feed him, he acted as though her milk was sour."

It hurt, this news. It spoke of such malice from her father's tribesmen, the same malice she heard in this girl's voice, that she felt it in her chest. Alaysha spurred the mount closer to the last trailing rider.

"I am the witch," she said.

The girl squirmed against her, awkwardly, but continued speaking as though Alaysha had said nothing.

"They say the witch can drink a man's soul."

"I wouldn't find it so tasty. Most men's souls are bitter."

"They say the witch kills without care."

"I've been trained as a warrior. All warriors are trained to kill without care."

"They say the witch feasts on the eyes of the men she has killed and answers only to Yuri."

"What is left of the eyes when I'm done would make a poor meal, and what daughter does not mind her father, especially if that father is the great Yuri—Conqueror of the Hordes."

The girl fell silent, digesting the information in place of the food her stomach grumbled for. Alaysha had never heard those notions about herself in such condensed terms before, nor had she been given an opportunity to answer to them. Propaganda that had no doubt been spread by Yuri himself.

Chapter 15

It was midday before Alaysha could see the white stone tower of Sarum's main gate through the trees. Her stomach burned with hunger. All the better to get the deed done, all the quicker. She expected Edulph to show soon. She reined in.

"We stop here," she shouted ahead to the men.

The train halted. Several of the men turned in their saddles, surprised to hear her speak.

The first, the one who appeared to be in charge, trotted back. He reined close to her mount.

"We do as Edulph bids."

"Edulph is not here."

"He wants us at the gates. He wants Yuri to see that one." He nodded at Bronwyn.

"To what end?"

"In case you are not what the tales tell."

"You think Yuri will trade his entire realm for one girl?"

"His daughter."

"A daughter—a thousand daughters—are nothing to Yuri."

"Then you better hope you're all the tales say you are."

Alaysha stared at him directly. "The tales are weak fairy stories told to fiddling children compared to what I am."

He blinked and tried to meet her gaze, but she could tell the vehemence of her tone shook him.

"I want to see Aedus. And then I want Aedus and Bronwyn to be saddled on this horse and sent two leaguas away."

"Edulph will never agree."

"You've gone to all this trouble to balk at one demand? You better find Edulph and see he gets my message."

The man turned his mount and Alaysha got off. She helped Bronwyn down.

"The witch has the spirit of three men, so they say," the girl said.

Alaysha smiled down at her and her throat felt tight. If she couldn't get this girl far enough away, she would never be able to live with herself.

She noticed the men around her had all dismounted and gone quiet. She followed their gazes off into the deep brush. Edulph, filthy from top to bottom with mud, strode from the thickest part. He had a leash of leather wrapped around his companion's neck. She noted Aedus's hair was hanging in her face and that she favored one hand, holding it close to her chest.

Alaysha had to force herself not to run to her. "Aedus," she said.

The girl looked up and the relief in her face was striking and quick and just as rapidly filled with regret.

"I'm sorry, Alaysha," Aedus said.

Edulph strode forward and faced Alaysha. "So. Aedus tells me you can drain a man without touching him. That you can empty the water from sealed vessels. You can bring rain."

She could do so much more, but if this was all he believed, she'd not correct him. She nodded. "All but that one thing. I cannot bring rain. It comes of its own."

"I don't care for the rain anyway." He pulled at the leash and Aedus jolted forward. "You will do this for me?"

"I will do it for Aedus."

He seemed satisfied. "I want my people out first. They're not to be harmed."

"I can't promise that."

"Then I'll have to persuade you." He yanked on the leash again and Aedus fell. She didn't whimper, but she stole a look from beneath her eyelids that bade Alaysha pay attention. The girl made a quick motion with her free hand, making a V with her fingers and sweeping them across her eyes. Alaysha made a quick decision.

"If you want your people safe, then call for them. But first you must get these two girls away from danger."

He took a few minutes to think, and Alaysha assumed he was considering all his options. She tried to make out if he had any strange residue beneath his eyes, but she couldn't tell from where she stood.

"What are you afraid of? That a few of your men can't watch over two young girls while a woman does your killing?"

He punished her by yanking on the leather leash so hard, Aedus bobbed forward, her hand going to her throat. "I fear nothing."

"And yet you need a small girl to protect you." Alaysha shook her head. She looked at him levelly. "I care nothing for Yuri's people or yours. I only care for Aedus and the girl. You have nothing to fear from me; it matters not one whit what happens to the people who enslaved my mother."

"But you wouldn't have killed those slavers unless I forced you?"

She shrugged. "I don't care if they live or die. Why would I care to kill them?"

"And you do have the power?"

"I do."

He turned to his first in command. "Take Yuri's daughter and tell him we have his witch. Deliver the message that if we do not have our people released by sunset, she will kill everyone within. If you are attacked, kill the girl. If you are not back before sunset, we will know you for dead and will attack whether our people are freed or not." He directed his attention to Alaysha.

"If the girl returns, you will do battle at dark."

"And if she doesn't return?"

"You will do battle at dark."

Alaysha nodded. She watched as the man hoisted Bronwyn onto the front of his mount. She knew Bronwyn would get into the gate fine, but whether she would get to Yuri was another matter.

She was about to speak to the girl, to offer her words of comfort if she could, when there was a shout from behind the group and several curses that stopped the riders and caught the crew's attention. The few words Alaysha didn't understand told her exactly who the person was that they'd caught in the bushes.

Yenic was pulled forward out of the underbrush by two men and Alaysha thought her lungs would not expand when she saw him. His hair was still loosed and muddy but with the addition of leaves and twigs stuck here and there. His eyes were no longer swollen, but held the mad look of someone who'd witnessed too many horrors to live through. So. The visions had stolen him after all. She felt incredibly sad.

Edulph found it all very funny. "Ah, the lover returns," he said.

Yenic stared around him, seeming to take in everything, but being able to respond to nothing. Alaysha guessed the visions still had him. She had to smother a groan. Now there would be far too many people she cared about to consider while she tried to end this game. Why couldn't he just have stayed where she left him?

Yenic blabbered a stream of incoherent words. He dodged at the air as though it held a demon trying to strike at him, but the holds his captors had on his arms just made him strain all the harder.

It would have been pathetic if Alaysha didn't feel such pain over his condition.

She looked at Edulph. "Let him go. He's far past harming you now."

Edulph snorted. "He was unable to harm me before." He motioned that the rider and Brownwyn should set out, and Alaysha watched the young girl staring over her captor's shoulder, her mouth agape at the strangeness of this man and the green streaks beneath his eyes. She craned around the man's shoulder until they were both out of sight.

Yenic tried to bolt for the bushes, but Greetha made a grab for him.

Edulph pulled at Aedus's leash. "You certainly smeared a lot of slime worm on him, sister. Thank you."

Alaysha thought she caught a blaze of anger behind Aedus's eyes before her gaze was cast downward and she smirked.

Edulph motioned for Yenic to be released and Alaysha crept over to him to touch his shoulder. "It's me, Yenic, " she cooed. "It's Alaysha. We're back at the oasis, now. Can you see it?"

It took a few seconds while he stared off into the air before he nodded passively. "Meroshi is no longer here."

"Good," she soothed. "Good. Why don't we go gather some peaches for supper. The tree is full." She led him gently away from the gang toward the lofty ditch in front of the city walls, knowing the rest of the men would settle into the shadows of the trees as they waited for dusk.

It would be a long wait before they knew the result of Bronwyn's visit. She found a good-sized tree root to settle on once they were a few kubits from the city's entrance. The rest of the men found their own spots—a good distance from the witch, she noticed.

She smiled to herself.

"What are you doing here?" She demanded of him once they were out of earshot.

He sat cross-legged beside her, making a show of it being awkward and maddened, but she knew better. He smelled of manure and mud and some other thing she couldn't name. Nothing ever smelled as sweet.

"I am the Witch's Arm," he said.

She took him in: his ribcage was less swollen and the cut above his brow had scabbed over, but the bruises were still purple and his breathing was labored. "Some Arm," she said. "How?"

"Barruch found me. I was… quite mad when he did, but I recognized him. I let him bring me to you." He leaned closer so his shoulder touched hers. "Alaysha. You can't kill Yuri."

"I can't now," she said. "If I kill Yuri, I kill you too."

He shook his head and put his hand on hers. She felt a tingle, like a charge of lightening had gone off beneath her skin

"I mean, you can't kill Yuri. He has your blood. He's protected. Even if you killed everyone, Yuri would still live and he would hunt you for betrayal."

She remembered all the times Yuri was not afraid when she let loose the power. It all made sense now. Not that it mattered.

"I'd have nothing to live for then, anyway."

"Alaysha, you are the most powerful witch of your kind. You have the culmination of dying generations in your blood."

"All the more reason for Yuri to end me."

"You are young," he said. "And ignorant."

She put her arm around him and squeezed, but angrily. "Then tell me, oh, Great Arm. What bits of wisdom do you have that can protect me, even from myself." Her tone and its fury surprised her.

He ignored her anger. "You need to get inside the walls and talk to Yuri."

"I thought Yuri was your enemy."

He gave her a queer look. "I am Yuri's enemy. That's not the same thing."

"It still changes nothing. Aedus, my sister, now you. To protect you, I kill. To refuse to kill, means you suffer harm. Either from Yuri or Edulph. One is the same as the other. War is war."

"This is not war, Alaysha. It's slaughter." His voice was pleading, and she didn't dare look at him for fear they would give themselves away if she did.

"Who is your worst enemy right now, Alaysha? Your father and his tribe or Edulph? Who is the worst?"

She thought about it. She remembered the way her father touched the heir's head, the fact that he saved its mother from a violent home and brought her to a place where she was revered. He was Yuri, Conqueror of the Hordes: fierce, unapologetic, but he was not evil. Cruel, yes, but not completely black-hearted.

Edulph would not spare his own sister pain to get what he wanted. And that decided her.

"I need to get into the city before dusk—before Edulph can find out what Yuri does to his emissary, Bronwyn or no."

"Yuri would let her die?"

She shrugged. "If they even made it past the gatekeepers and she still lives, Yuri would think first of the whole city."

"Even if it works, Alaysha, Edulph still won't let Aedus go."

"I know that."

He thought for a moment. "I'll get to her then."

"By sunset. I think she marked Edulph; I don't know how she managed it, but I think she did and he should be about ready to undergo the same hell you just did."

He chuckled. "I suppose everyone has to sleep sometime. Maybe she convinced him to eat some and saved a few to grind down while he wasn't looking."

Alaysha smiled to herself. The girl was clever. She hoped the cleverness stuck with her for a while yet, but if it didn't, and she was gone...

"If you can't get to her in time, run. Don't linger, because I will loose all the power I can to reach to the very pit of Edulph's soul. I swear it."

"I'll wait for you, Alaysha. Until the end of it."

She couldn't kiss him there in front of them all, but she could touch him, and she did. She grasped his hand and prayed to the Deities he wouldn't let her go.

Chapter 16

Sarum was the largest village within weeks of a horse's full gallop, and it lay in a crevice against a mountain of white stone with a broad river on one side and a dense forest on the other. The only place left open was a funnel of land that was flat and open. The city itself was surrounded by a reverse ditch with several small mottes stretching across it at strategic places and a main gate in the middle. Yuri had designed the village so the main keep lay in the center and wooden buildings created a maze around it. The only reliable way in was through the gate and past the death hole just behind it.

Alaysha found no resistance as she approached the entrance. Any kind of reception, she knew, would be beyond the wall within the death hole. Yuri had used the labor of captives over the last decade to build a dwelling for himself of solid white stone from quarries across his land. The stones were mortared together by a paste of clay mixed with the starchy glue of a sticky grain they threshed in the fall. It wasn't solid so much as it was flexible, letting the stone stand and move against battering rams or scaling ladders. It also meant it was guarded heavily so that the vertical slits could be re-manned by archers as quickly as they went down.

The question was whether Bronwyn had delivered her message and what Yuri had done when she did. That would decide what greeted her when she unwound the gate. There could be a hundred guards ready to burst through, or the entire city could already be retreating through the south gate into the woods beyond. It was even possible Edulph's people were lined up at the gate waiting to be loosed. Possible, but highly unlikely.

She looked up for signs of the guard. Nothing. The sky was still blue, but turning to indigo at the edges. In a few moments, it would begin to bleed to pink and then to crimson, and then the sun would be gone.

She sent her thirst out ahead of her, searching for water. She tasted stagnant well, skins filled with leathery water, the odd bit of moisture within mushrooms hidden in parts of cellars. She searched for sweat next, and tears. Blood. There was precious little of the first two, quite a bit of the last.

She chewed her lip and looked for the handle to open the door. She took a breath and grasped the lever, grunting at the effort and only managing to swing the door open enough to squeeze inside.

What she expected was not what met her. At first quick glance, the death hole was empty and obviously meant to appear so. She turned just to the right where she knew a platform had been erected for archers. It was empty of warriors save one.

Edulph's emissary was dangling by one foot from the top. His eyes stared forward in death.

It was the low hum that really caught her attention and when she looked to the left, there, all piled like refuse, lay hundreds of bodies. All raggedly dressed, filthy. The dregs of the slave quarters. The laborers. The ones who were used to cut trees and lug stones to keep the wall fires fed. All would have been Edulph's people, she knew. Yuri had elected to kill them rather than give in to the demands.

So. It was obvious his message had been received and not been appreciated.

She scanned the area, holding her breath against the smell of defecation and urine that had been the last living task of self-preservation. She refused to look at the two dogs rooting in the pile of bodies or the rat that scuttled from one corner of the wall to burrow beneath. Instead, she turned to the sky. It was turning pink. She hoped Yenic got Edulph by now and had managed to free Aedus. Whether or not he had, it would not matter soon enough.

"They say the witch cares for nothing."

Alaysha couldn't believe she was hearing the voice. She whirled around to see Bronwyn standing next to the well, her hand touching the pail.

"Thank the Deities," she said. It took her a moment to realize the girl didn't seem afraid. "Are you okay?"

Bronwyn nodded.

Alaysha was confused. "What happened here?"

The girl looked at the man hanging from the rafters of the platform. "It would seem our father does care for daughters."

"He had him killed to save you?" Alaysha had to know.

Bronwyn's expression softened. "Maybe. But I think he died because he dared oppose Yuri."

Alaysha waved at the pile of dead laborers. "And these?"

"To show Edulph how we feel about being opposed."

"Where's Yuri?"

At that, Bronwyn cast a nervous glance to her left. It was so quick, Alaysha might doubt she'd seen it except for the shadow that moved in the portico and then stilled.

"Do you oppose your father, Witch?"

Before Alaysha could answer the voice behind her, she felt the air stir, and the hot feeling of wetness streaming down her hip. She looked down at herself. Blood. So much of it. She placed her hand on her waist, looking for the source, and then the pain came, and then the fear came with it.

She thought she heard her father shout, and Bronwyn let go a shriek. She thought she saw Drahl dance in front of her, his sword held aloft, ready to strike again, but it was too late to see more or to assess much else.

The thirst had already come, and her mouth filled with the taste of his sweat. She saw the paths to his moisture and collected it so fast he collapsed in front of her, stiff, hard, a leathered husk without eyes to see what he'd done. She was already tasting the tears from Bronwyn's face, the liquid in the blood that drove from her heart to her throat.

She tried to stop it. She tried to picture her nohma, Aedus, Yenic, anyone she had any real connection to. She worked hard to bring some memory of love to her mind, but all that came was the stagnant water left in the leathered skins, the cold water from the well.

Her stomach was on fire, and all she could think was that she had to put it out, and even as she fell to her knees, she could see the droplets gathering above the well into a cloud of mist, ready to come to her bidding.

She felt someone's hands on her belly, pressing hard. She tried to focus on the face: Bronwyn. Her face working to shed tears that had already been pulled from her. Yuri's stern mouth yelling, his hands beneath her head.

"Stop it," he demanded. "You're killing Bronwyn."

Bronwyn. Aedus. Yenic. Nohma. Nohma and her stories. Nohma sewing garnets into her bridal tunic. Nohma kissing her forehead and singing her to sleep after battle with songs of some place called Etlantium that her mother loved. Her mother. Never known but for that one second when she saw the sea green color of her eyes in that one instant before the memory went black.

Finally, all she could taste was the blood from her own mouth, and she knew she'd been able to stop the power. She hoped it wasn't too late, that her struggles to contain it had at least kept it from accelerating.

"It's over," she heard her father say, and she looked up at the sky to see the crimson edged clouds block out the last of the sun.

She couldn't help a weak smile. Yes. All over soon.

The hands on her stomach had gone and she could make out the scuffling sound of footsteps in the dirt. There was an exclamation of surprise from Yuri and a demand to lower a weapon. Then: Yenic's voice? Cocky. Saying he was not a mere number. Bronwyn begging for a poor madman's life.

Someone pressed again on her stomach.

"She's gone for the shaman." Yuri's voice. Bronwyn, he must mean.

"Don't you dare let her die," she heard. Was it Yenic? Or Yuri? She couldn't tell anymore, just felt hands on her belly, pressing down hard. She wanted to tell them both it didn't matter. Soon she couldn't be used anymore— not by her father, not by Edulph. Balance could come when she was gone. She couldn't speak and her eyelids felt so heavy, all she wanted to do was close them. She thought of all the seeds she'd collected, hoping someday she could find a way to grow them back into men. It was childish. A fantasy. She should have known the only way she could undo what she'd done was to undo herself.

She felt herself go, and sent a silent thanks to her nohma's deities for taking away the pain of living. She thought she felt the first drops of rain.

Chapter 17

Yenic's voice, mingled with Yuri's, was the sound she heard when she returned. Arguing. Yenic's patient tone against Yuri's steely cold one.

"He's even madder now than before." She heard Yenic say and in her cloud of confusion, it seemed natural to hear both of those voices in the same proximity.

"If she'd not brought him here, we wouldn't have to concern ourselves." Was Yuri's reply. So he was angry at her for bringing Edulph. She didn't blame him, but why would he be discussing it with the hated number nineteen?

She rolled her head to the side and breathed. She smelled smoke and boiled poultry. She no longer lay on the earth, but felt the cushion of goose feathers and linen beneath her back, the weight of a soft linen and fur atop her. Her stomach felt numb and she reached down to feel for the wound she knew was there. Her fingers came away sticky.

"It's honey."

With some effort, she was able to open her eyes.

Bronwyn sat next to her. On quick scan, Alaysha could tell they were in one of the wooden buildings mazing the Main Keep; she guessed it was the young wife's home. She sat in the corner cooing to a bundle of linens. So it seemed Alaysha had not killed the heir after all. She was surprised that she felt nothing at the awareness and realized she was probably drugged.

"The shaman sewed you shut and bandaged you," Bronwyn said. "He says the honey will keep away the green death."

"I'm not dead, then."

Bronwyn broke a smile. "Nearly. Drahl wasn't supposed to do that." She hid her eyes behind a fringe of hair as she hung her head. "I'm sorry."

Alaysha tried to pat the girl's hand; she ended up merely poking at the top with weak fingers. It was coming more clearly now. Yuri and Yenic in the same room? These enemies? Someone would die. She tried to get up and intercept the bloodshed she knew would soon come, and a stab of pain shot through her.

"Yenic," she mumbled falling back onto her mattress.

"It's okay," Bronwyn said. "He and Father have a common enemy, it seems."

And so were reluctant allies.

"Aedus?" she asked, but was surprised that the sound was a mere whisper.

"Yenic was able to save her."

The relief stung her eyes and she had to close them to ease the pain.

It seemed her father and Yenic both realized she was awake at the same time, and both faces hovered above hers when she opened them again.

"Alaysha," Yenic said. "You're awake. Do you remember much? Do you feel strong again?"

Her father merely scowled at him. "Never mind if she feels strong." His tone held something that Alaysha might have called suspicion if she had to label it.

"This boy dares tell me you have been badly trained." He'd made some sort of peace with Yenic, but it was obvious he was unhappy about it.

"She does need training," Yenic said to Yuri. "I told you, the best defense is to teach her. Not to leave her ignorant."

Yuri straightened and squared off against Yenic, whose bruises were yellowed now instead of purple. "If it's as dire as you say, then you should be out there, not in here."

"And leave Alaysha alone with you."

"She's been with me her eighteen years," Yuri said. "You see harm in her staying longer?"

Bronwyn hovered over her. "They've been fighting since Father allowed Yenic to live."

Alaysha could only guess why. "Edulph survived."

The girl nodded. "Went mad, according to Aedus, and ran off into the woods shouting at things that weren't there."

"What kinds of things?"

"Witches that breathe fire, that make the earth shake."

Her words caught Yenic's attention and Yuri stood watching his reaction with a narrowed gaze. Yenic rushed to the bedside.

"Witches, Alaysha. Do you know what that means?"

"It means we are in even more danger now," Yuri said. He took in Alaysha's face and made a hard line with his lips. She could only imagine what he was thinking.

Yenic ignored him. "You were made powerful because you received your grandmother and mother's unused power at the same time. It peaks as you age, and wanes too. It collects, waiting to be uncoiled. When your grandmother died, and your mother, you inherited the culmination of all that available waiting power. It doubled, tripled in you." He glared at Yuri. "Your father knew this and used it."

"And you wouldn't?" Yuri said to him and Yenic held the icy gaze until the baby squalled and Yuri rushed to the corner to take it from its mother.

"Nohma?" Alaysha had to know. If she was protected, then why had she died?

Yenic sighed. "No one could know your power was too much for her as you grew older. It seems even a blood witch is not safe when the power coils so tightly or when the blood is too far from the source."

"What of Drahl?" she asked, touching her side.

Yuri stepped forward, all bluster and outrage. He had his hand cupped over the heir's head and Alaysha thought he'd squeeze the poor thing, so fierce was his tone.

"Drahl was a soldier to the last." His white hair was in disarray, as though he'd run greasy fingers through it repeatedly. She'd never seem him so restless.

She knew he wouldn't malign his scout; he'd rather believe he tried to kill in the Great Yuri's service rather than from hatred.

"Drahl is dead," Yenic said. "And Edulph lives. And if he was raving about the witches, then he knows of the others."

Yuri snorted and Alaysha had a hard time keeping him in focus, so much did he begin to pace about the room. She knew her brow was furrowing in confusion, but she didn't have the words to ask what she wanted. Yenic reached for her hand.

"My mother," he murmured. "And the earth witch. The first is powerful, yes, but the last was made as you were, and she is a babe yet."

"You said your tribe was gone."

He sent her a regretful smile. "I have to keep some secrets."

Another snort from Yuri, derisive, disbelieving.

She looked at her father, and said the first thing that came to her mind. "If Edulph finds the child, he'll try to control her." He glowered, but said nothing in his defense. In truth, he had begun to prowl about and went repeatedly to the corner of the room where his young wife sat. He eased the child into her arms and bid her leave.

"We can't let him reach either of the witches," he said, and looked pointedly at Yenic.

She closed her eyes. Everything hurt, and this news made it all seem worse. "I need to go," she said and Yenic put his hand on her shoulder when she tried to get up.

"You need to rest and heal. You're not useful in this shape."

"I'm better."

"Not better enough to be useful."

She sighed and Bronwyn laid a cool linen against her forehead. Alaysha tried to brush it away.

"We have to stop—"

Yuri's voice cut her off. "We will stop him. The bastard nearly had my whole city on the brink of death."

Alaysha took him in, from the long, untethered white hair to his steel blue eyes, and couldn't stop the question no matter how hard she tried. "Is that what has you so angry, Father? How does it feel?"

He glowered at her and turned to Yenic. "I will stop anyone who threatens me. You understand this?"

Yenic gave a brief nod.

"You are only alive because of Edulph. You know that, too?"

"You've already told me three times. If I didn't understand the first and second, surely one more time will help me."

Yuri grunted his satisfaction, but he didn't seem ready to give in. "If you do take Aedus and head out to find him, I want him brought here."

"I should go to my mother first."

"No." Yuri's voice was adamant. "Not alone. Not even with Aedus. You need the witch for that." With a deft movement, he pointed to Alaysha. She thought he'd forgotten she could hear.

"Perhaps I could bring my mother here. Alaysha should be trained."

Alaysha wasn't sure bringing more powerful women into Yuri's domain was a good idea. Yenic nodded as though it wasn't a concern at all. "Yes. First I'll go to my mother. Then we'll return for Alaysha."

Yuri shook his head. "Return for the witch? What does that mean?"

"To take her with us when we search for the babe. I'm sure you would want her properly trained if we find ourselves against an unpredictable and powerful child."

Yuri seemed to be considering and when he'd come to some sort of internal answer to his own raging debate, he spoke with authority. "She's unpredictable enough," he said, nodding toward Alaysha. "So, go. We'll care for her until you return."

She could have been a flank of venison the way he said it. She closed her eyes and felt the warmth of lips on her cheek; without looking, she knew they were Yenic's.

His voice fell to a whisper. "You're safe now. Rest and build your strength."

She burrowed deeper beneath the fur and let sleep take her.

Chapter 18

She woke to the sound of chirping birds, and the smell of fresh air coming in through an open window. Aedus was toddling around the room, picking items up and shoving them into a leather bag.

"Where have you been?"

The girl spun on her heel and dropped the bundle. "You don't remember."

Alaysha shook her head.

"I've been here since Yenic brought you in—all but for the first day when I was sent to the shaman." She lifted her hand and Alaysha noticed the place where the index finger had been severed had been seared closed and smoothed over. She winced, and Aedus grinned.

"It's okay. They gave me a draft: root of dreams the shaman said, while they cleaned it up. I slept like a dog after a big meal."

"I think I've sampled it myself." Alaysha tried to shift and sent pain streaking across her midsection.

"Don't move," the girl told her. "You don't want to split it open again."

"Again?"

The girl nodded.

"Where's Yenic?"

Aedus chewed her lip. "He's saddling Barruch."

"And you're going with him?"

The girl came closer. "Well, it's not like I was going to leave until I said goodbye."

Alaysha tried to smile, but she felt too lonely all of a sudden to do a good job of it.

"Don't worry, Alaysha. It's just a few days. You need to heal anyway, and we'll be back just when you're well enough to train."

"You sound like Yenic."

"He made me practice the words." The girl smoothed the fur over Alaysha's legs thoughtfully, then she brightened.

"I have a horse. Yenic demanded one for me."

"Yenic is commanding the great Yuri?"

"The great Yuri has become strangely cooperative."

Alaysha grunted at that news. She had wondered herself at the sudden shift in Yuri, and even though he was still surly, his surliness was still not typical.

"I can wait a few days, I suppose," she said.

She was left alone then, and she slept. Until Yuri came.

Like he had done before he left, he took to pacing around the room. Alaysha watched him for a few moments, could see that he was struggling with something. She thought it best to wait until he had formed his thoughts.

He finally turned her. "What did he tell you?"

"Who? Yenic?"

He nodded. "What did he tell you of your past?"

"He told me the truth. That his tribe has four clans. That each has its own powerful woman and each of those has support you never gave me."

"You had your mother's sister."

"Not for long."

"Is that my fault?" He settled next to her and his expression shifted into something she'd never seen on him except for when he looked at his heir. She wanted to believe it had something to do with her being wounded, but she knew better.

"He told me why you wanted him dead."

He chuckled at that. "Did he?"

She watched his face for signs of alarm. She wasn't surprised when he showed nothing but condescension.

She had to retract her statement. "He only told me that I killed his grandmother and his sister and all of the other elders. I killed all of their Arms and all of their blood witches." She met his gaze. "But you know all of that. Because you sent me to do it."

"Did he ever say he was your Arm?" His expression was still unreadable.

She thought back over their time together. "No. He never said it."

"No," he agreed. "Because he isn't."

She was confused. It was true he had never said so, but she had assumed it, and he never corrected her.

"Did he ever protect you that you remember? Did he ever shield you with his body, make magic for you?"

She shook her head.

"It's because he can't. He is his mother's Arm."

His mother's Arm. So that meant he'd intentionally misled her—if her father could be believed.

"Why would he lie to me?"

"Why would I?"

She kept her his gaze until he lowered his first. "Yes," he said. "I do know that I stand to gain. I admit it. But he lied to you. I never did. I've never lied."

If he hadn't lied, it was only because he didn't care enough to pretend for her, she thought. When she didn't respond, he continued, pressing it seemed because he felt he needed to, that he sensed her reluctant belief.

"He didn't tell you about the others. Did he? And yet he knew about them, he knew they were still alive. How did he manage to survive your thirst? How was he able to survive when you were able to kill three fully gifted crones? Have you asked yourself that?"

She couldn't answer. She'd never once given it a thought. One thing stood out to her, though; Yenic's aversion to killing Yuri and slaughtering the innocent people within Sarum. She held to that, she had to keep believing in that. It was the one thing that could dispel her father's reasoning.

"What are you implying?"

"You know what I'm implying."

"But it doesn't make sense; if he wanted Sarum he could have had it."

"Sarum is a small thing really. To you and me, a large thing, but to someone with other motives…" He shrugged.

"But why would he ask me not to attack you, Father? Why would he speak of slaughter rather than war? Why would he defend you?" She felt the warmth of Yenic's words of safety, of his kiss, all slipping away and she was desperate to recover it.

A smile snaked over Yuri's face and for a second, Alaysha believed him far more clever than she'd ever thought.

"Control doesn't have to be an overt thing," he said, and she had the grey shifting thought that she'd heard it somewhere before. "If I had ever asked you to stay your hand, what would you have thought of me?"

She considered that. She had been willing to let him die because he'd always used her. Would she have been as willing if he'd ever shown kindness to his targets, treated them like people instead of objects? If he'd ever given consideration for how she would feel about killing?

"It would be harder to see you as an object," is what she said.

He nodded. "And an object can be done harm much easier than can a person, no matter how cruel. Isn't that what you were taught? To feel nothing when you killed? To imagine the warriors as targets and not as men?

"What if those old women in the village were not the others," he asked. "Or if they were, what if they were not there of their free will?"

"But--"

"How were you manipulated?"

She considered it. "Aedus. Bronwyn. Yenic too."

He nodded. "What if those crones truly were the real witches who had loved ones held captive somewhere?"

She hadn't considered that either. She tried to picture Yenic with his honeyed gaze and find deception in it. She found all she could do was see him suffering from the dreamer's worm, the swelling he bore from trying to save Aedus, the way his mouth looked when he wanted to kiss her.

That last made her chest tight with anger. If he'd deceived her, he'd used a most vile way to do it.

"He says you're untrained, and maybe in your gift, you are, but I trained you well no matter what he says. Use what I have given you—harden your heart like I taught you so you can't be treated as a tool against your will. It's the best way."

"So, what if he did lie to me, Father; I killed his sister. Her unborn child. All for you." She felt the strength of her argument weakening in the reality of her father's steely stare.

"You are so young, Witch. You see only what's in front of you while other men see far and beyond. Have you thought about what would happen if a man could control all the elements? Water, fire, earth, air? Have you?"

She looked him over, trying to read what was unreadable in him. "It depends on the man."

He sighed. "I didn't get to be Emir of Sarum by trusting anyone, or from being kind."

He passed her a draft of warm liquid: dreamer's root, she supposed, and she took large gulps of it. Everything had seemed so simple before and now it had turned more complex than she could manage. All she wanted was sleep. Her stomach burned. Her mind burned. Worst of all, her chest burned as though someone had reached inside and set fire to a secret place within.

"I don't know if I'm the right man," Yuri said to her, "But at least I can say I wanted to prevent a war that might finish us all off, and if it comes to our threshold anyway, I will fight it." His last words were passion-filled, and Alaysha had to struggle to keep his gaze under the fire of his words.

"And this is what you didn't tell me before. Why you wanted Yenic and Yenic's tribe dead." She could hear the slur in her words as the drug took effect, and she fought to keep her eyes open, her ears capable of hearing his answer.

"Better to have the only witch when you can't have them all, than to let someone else control the most of them."

She wanted to believe Yenic could be trusted, but there were too many questions now to simply believe him on faith. Her stomach squirmed as she thought about him and his touch—how it had felt lying next to him in the dark—and she started to feel the sure pangs of anger and hurt. How could he have done such a thing to her? She'd been foolish and ignorant, and even young, as he'd kept telling her she was. He'd used her more foully than her father had ever done.

But could she trust her father either? Best she do like Yuri: keep her own counsel and trust only her own motives because those were the only ones she could fully know. She would never be used again against her will: not by Yuri, and certainly not by Yenic. Especially not Yenic.

She was so tired, far more tired than weariness or dreamer's draft could ever account for. She watched her father wait for her to close her eyes, and when she did, she heard him move across the cabin and out the door. She fought to open her eyes, to be sure he'd gone and that she was alone. Only then did she feel relieved enough to let go the tears that burned in her eyes, and when she was done, she felt more certain. No matter what came, she knew she could trust herself and herself alone.

For the present, though, she'd lie here and listen to the birds and thank the Deities that for now, that was all they were—songbirds celebrating the day, and not carrion vultures shrieking over an unexpected and unnatural meal. That might come another day, but it wasn't now; it wouldn't be today.

She closed her eyes again and let the birdsong send her to sleep.

Continue the saga with *Blood Witch*

More from the Witches of Etlantium (Available in Kindle and other formats)
Seeds of the Soul
Water Witch book 1

Blood Witch book 2
Bone Witch book 3
Breath Witch book 4
Theron's Tale
Sons of Alkaia:

CPSIA information can be obtained
at www.ICGtesting.com
Printed in the USA
BVOW06s1145220517
484835BV00008B/55/P